"Come on, Becky! What's Dan Simmons *really* like?"

Becky glanced around the cafeteria, then back at Sarah. "What do you mean?" Playing dumb would give her another minute to think.

Sarah rolled her eyes. "Give me a break, Becky. You *know* what I mean! What's DOS *really* like?"

"DOS?" Becky arched an eyebrow at her friend.

"Yeah, Dan Simmons." Sarah leaned back. "We just found out his middle initial is *O*. Get it? DOS—disk operating system. Pretty appropriate, huh?"

Becky laughed. It *was* an appropriate set of initials for the company's resident computer expert.

"So fill me in," Sarah insisted. "We all want to find out more about Dan Simmons. Ever since he started here, he's pretty much kept to himself—almost as if he's hiding something."

"That's ridiculous!" Becky said firmly. And yet...there *were* a few things that didn't add up.

Marie DeWitt lives in Minnesota with her husband, three sons aged eleven, twelve and fourteen, two dogs and three cats—a busy household, as she says. She's a high school teacher who's always wanted to write; her husband's a minister who's also a computer director. He encourages Marie's writing, taught her about computers—and even bought her a printer when *Daniel's Deception* was finished! Not surprisingly, this story is dedicated to him....

DANIEL'S DECEPTION

Marie DeWitt

WORLDWIDE®

TORONTO • NEW YORK • LONDON
AMSTERDAM • PARIS • SYDNEY • HAMBURG
STOCKHOLM • ATHENS • TOKYO • MILAN
MADRID • WARSAW • BUDAPEST • AUCKLAND

Special thanks and acknowledgment to
Marie DeWitt

ISBN 0-373-83284-2

DANIEL'S DECEPTION

One

Daniel O. Simmons stopped tapping the keyboard just long enough to give his black-framed glasses a little shove back into place.

It had been a long day, a grueling day. To the average businessman, it was the kind of day that can't end soon enough. The kind of day that calls for a good brandy to put it all in perspective.

But to Daniel, this day was the stuff of dreams. Because Daniel absolutely *loved* his work. As Information Systems manager—or resident computer expert—for an insurance company, he'd been putting in twelve-hour days for the past month.

And as if that wasn't enough, he spent his "free" time creating computer programs.

It was a secret to many that Dan had been born with a silver spoon in his mouth and had not discovered computers until the age of thirty. He'd taken to them like a cowboy takes to the local saloon girl after months of celibacy. Now, at the age of thirty-five, Dan was one of the most respected computer directors in the state. Though employed by a small company, he was often called in to troubleshoot for other firms in the area.

Dan gave his glasses another firm push, then returned his fingers to the keyboard. Just a few more minutes, and he'd be through. Much as he'd enjoyed his day with all its challenges, he was looking forward to going home; tonight, he was going to finish his first computer game. He hoped to sell it to an international toy company.

He smiled with genuine satisfaction. A new computer game was about to be born—one that had been nurtured under his watchful eye. Life couldn't get any better than that.

The shrill ring of the phone interrupted his work. He raked his hand through his sandy hair and grabbed the receiver.

"Dan Simmons."

"Dan? This is Becky."

"Hello." Dan cradled the receiver on his shoulder as he exited his own computer program. "Problems?"

Becky cleared her throat. "Well, yes."

"What is it?" he asked, stifling a sigh. Problems in the secretarial department were nothing new. The secretaries ran into computer problems more often than stock car drivers dented their vehicles. "What is it?" He repeated the clipped question, revealing his impatience at being disturbed.

"Uh, could you come down here for a minute?" Becky asked nervously.

Dan groaned inwardly as he glanced at the clock. For once, he didn't want to stay late. There were only fifteen minutes left of the workday. However, he could probably take care of their problems in that time. Then again, he might not be able to. They were notorious for jamming up the works. If it was anyone else, Dan would wait until tomorrow. But he admired Becky's efficiency and knew that if she was calling him at this time of day, it must be important.

"I'll be right there." He replaced the receiver and shut down his own terminal. He began the trek to the second floor and to the secretarial pool—the remedial room, as he privately called it.

As he entered the spacious room, he surveyed the scene. Fourteen terminals sat back-to-back in two rows. Fourteen terminals—which usually meant a *hundred* and fourteen problems. No, a *thousand* and fourteen. No, *ten thousand* and...

Becky motioned to Dan to join her at the very last computer. Her signal was unnecessary, he thought. She stood out from the others. In a room filled with young women, every latest fashion statement was made. But not by Becky. Ever since Dan had known her, she had ignored the fashion trends, preferring sedate business suits or conservative dresses. Navy blue seemed to be her color.

Today was no different. As he walked over to her, he noted her straight, below-the-knee navy skirt with matching jacket. She had unbuttoned the jacket, revealing a tailored white shirt with a crisp collar. Despite her staid, almost old-fashioned appearance, the rest of the women respected her because she had the fastest typing speed this side of the Mississippi. They were right; he'd seen her in action.

Dan didn't care how she looked. He never noticed a woman's appearance. Well, maybe that wasn't quite true. He noticed women all right; appreciated them as much as the next guy. Their hair, their eyes, their legs—especially their legs... But he didn't have the time or the energy to spend on getting to *know* a woman. There was just too much to do. While most young, single men spent their Saturday evenings out on the town, Dan was usually holed up in his apartment researching the latest computer technology or working on his game. He was busy enjoying his newfound freedom and anonymity, and that included freedom from countless social obligations. The fewer people who knew his background, the better.

He made his way toward Becky, glancing at her shapely legs—what he could see of them. One thing about Becky: she had legs that wouldn't quit. He'd sure like to discover the feel of them for himself.... Dan was perturbed by the direction of his thoughts. He didn't have the time or interest to pursue a relationship, he reminded himself. Not at this point in his life, anyway.

Becky smiled as he approached. She had a lovely smile that seemed to light up the already bright room. Some of the secretaries considered Becky a tough supervisor, but Dan didn't agree. In his experience with her, Becky had always seemed reasonable. She was a woman highly committed to her job and to the company. It was evident in everything she did. Her call tonight was a good example. She preferred to deal with a situation immediately. He liked that.

Dan admired the way her long blond hair was neatly held in place by side combs. When she turned, he noticed how it fell in waves down to the middle of her back. He also noticed, as though for the first time, how dainty she looked. Old-fashioned word, dainty. It suited her.

Six feet tall himself, Dan towered over her. Suddenly he itched to touch those small pink-nailed hands; he wanted to feel her skin to see if it was as smooth as it looked. The pearl shirt buttons caught his attention and he followed them— up, up—to the collar that was buttoned primly at her slender neck.

What would it be like to gently unfasten those buttons, kissing her neck, touching her with soft kisses as he made his way lower and lower? His dark brown eyes darkened as they met her cornflower-blue ones. The contact shocked him back to reality. What was the matter with him? Soon, all too soon, his pilgrimage would be over, and he'd be forced to return to California. And he couldn't subject a woman like Becky to his life-style there. She was the type of woman who probably wanted to live in peace and serenity, with a white picket fence, two kids and a dog. A normal, ordinary life. And that was something he could never give her; he could never give it to anyone.

Dan experienced the old familiar twinge of disappointment. As the only heir to the Simmons Corporation, there'd been expectations placed upon him. In fact, with the death of his father a few years ago, the expectations had become an albatross, choking every bit of life from him until he couldn't stand it. So he'd taken off and wound up in Minneapolis, Minnesota, in a normal job with a normal routine. Keeping his identity a secret was wonderful. For the first time in his life, people knew him for the person he was, for his values, his beliefs, his skills, and not as an appendage of an extremely wealthy family. He wanted it to remain this way for as long as possible. For that reason, he knew he had to avoid personal entanglements. And *especially* with a woman like Becky who obviously valued privacy. He knew very well that a romance was out of the question. Now, if his body would only cooperate! Becky was, to put it simply, one good-looker.

She licked her lips nervously when her eyes met Dan's. He was so handsome! Ever since he'd come to work here, she'd noticed him. As he gazed at her, Becky found her mouth going dry. Lord, he was tall! For a man who spent his days at a desk, he certainly had a good build. Even his two-piece, well-pressed brown suit couldn't hide his physique. He always dressed impeccably. Today he wore an off-white shirt with a brown-striped tie. His wavy hair was brushed perfectly into place, the ends of his hair just touching the top of his collar.

He was leaning over her desk, frowning, as he studied her computer screen. He smelled clean and masculine, with a hint of some woodsy after-shave. His long fingers tapped on her keyboard, and the action drew her attention to his gold watch and the onyx ring on his right hand. No, he wasn't married; she knew that. The whole company knew that! She wasn't the only woman who'd been swept away by his good looks.

However, Becky was the only woman who knew this man was out of her league. She sighed. For one thing, he was thirty-five, which made him ten years older than her. And there was something about him. Something hard to define, hard to pin down... And if that wasn't enough to stop her fantasies, all she had to do was remember her disastrous past and her mother's warnings.

Dan Simmons had his pick of women. He'd never even give her the time of day. And if he ever found out the truth, found out what had happened to her, she'd be lucky if he remembered she was alive.

He studied the display on the screen, then asked, "What's the problem?"

Becky forced a smile, dismissing her errant thoughts. "We, uh, can't seem to exit this program," she began as she pushed a lock of hair behind her ear.

Dan was quiet for a minute. "Did you follow my directions on that sheet I handed out?" Silence. She was staring at her feet. "Becky, did you hear what I said?"

"Yes," she replied faintly, gripping the back of her chair.

She licked her lips again. Dan saw the action and experienced a tightening in his stomach.

She raised her eyes to his. As supervisor, she'd called on him any number of times. But today was different somehow. *He* was different somehow.

She swallowed before she said again, softly, "Yes, I did, but I think I need you to explain a few things to me."

Dan leaned over and quickly pushed a couple of keys. Within seconds, the program was gone and the main menu displayed. "Sure," he said distractedly as he shut down the terminal.

Becky glanced at her watch. "Oh, I didn't mean right now. It's almost five. How about when you have a few moments in the next day or so?"

Dan watched her silently. For a woman a few years out of college, she handled herself very professionally. Although he was determined to ignore the attraction he felt for her he'd made it his business to find out as much as he could. I had been easy—he'd just listened to gossip in the lunch room.

Becky Thorpe, age twenty-five, lived alone in a small downtown apartment. She'd graduated summa cum laude with a degree in business and took this job three years ago Dan could see that she performed her job flawlessly, bu kept to herself except for Sarah Swan, who worked over in Accounting.

And from Sarah, he'd managed to learn—by way of casual questioning—that Becky was originally from Eaton, Minnesota, a small farming community north of the Twin Cities. She had only one living relative—her mother, who still lived in the farmhouse that Becky grew up in.

So Dan had all the superficial information that he needed. But he realized he wanted more. Why was she such a loner? Why wasn't she married? Did she date? If so, who? Did she like classical music, soft rock or jazz? What was her favorite food? And why did she look as if she hid some inner sadness? All right, so he *was* interested in her. There. He'd admitted it. Maybe it was time to act. The computer game didn't seem so important tonight, after all. Besides, he rationalized, their relationship could be strictly platonic, couldn't it?

Nonchalantly he glanced at his watch. "It is five, isn't it?" He cupped his chin in his hand. "How about a hamburger across the street, while I tell you about the program?"

Dan watched as she considered his suggestion. Frowning, she bit the tip of her nail. Why was she so uncomfortable? He'd only suggested an informal, impromptu meal. What was she afraid of? Him? He didn't think so. Yet if he was a good judge of character—and he believed he was—he'd say she definitely seemed uneasy.

Dan didn't like the fact that he apparently made her nervous. He wanted her to relax with him; yes, dammit, he wanted to get to know her better. Irritably, he jammed his hand into his pants pocket.

Becky stared at him in disbelief. He was asking her to have supper with him? Okay, it was just a hamburger at the fast-food place across the street, but it had been a long time since any man had requested her company. Correction. It had been a long time since she'd *allowed* any man to request her company. It was just safer that way.

Until now. She thought about all the nights she ate alone. Suddenly she knew she wouldn't be able to bear another evening like that, not when she could be eating with a very exciting, attractive man. Even if it *was* work-related. One mistake in a person's life didn't mean she had to give up everything, did it? Besides, what harm was there in going out for a hamburger with the man? As long as she remembered that, things would be fine.

Becky's mind was made up. "Thank you. That sounds fine," she said resolutely. "Just let me grab my coat, all right?"

Dan nodded. "I'll meet you at the front entrance. I need to clean up my desk first."

"All right." Dan was treated to a smile. All of a sudden, he was filled with pleasure that he was the person who'd put that smile on her face. For a young woman, she sure didn't smile often. Maybe he could change that.

He hummed softly to himself as he returned to his office.

Becky was waiting for him when he arrived at the doorway. It was early October and the air was chilly, so she'd put on a dark blue coat that covered practically all of her. Where the hemline ended, her shoes peeked out. She clutched her navy shoulder bag as though it was a life jacket and she was about to board the *Titanic*. Dan wished he could put her at ease.

She watched him approach and tried not to stare. He was just a man, she reminded herself. Maybe if she said it often enough she would begin to believe it. Just a man? Dan Simmons embodied every aspect of masculinity she knew. Of course, this wasn't a true date. That knowledge gave her enough courage to continue with the evening. Because if it *was* a date, she'd have run as fast as she could in the opposite direction. Before anything else happened.

"Shall we?" Dan held the heavy glass door open for her, nodding her along.

"Thanks." She hadn't been reduced to one-word answers for a long time. Right now, though, one-word answers seemed all she could manage.

Crossing Second Avenue took hardly any time. In tense silence, they waited for the signal to change and walked toward the little restaurant. While traffic in downtown Minneapolis would be congested right now, here, in the suburb of Roseville, where the insurance company's offices were, things moved more slowly. Becky loved living in the Twin Cities. When she'd decided to relocate here, she had been delighted by all the concerts, plays and movies there were to see. By the museums, galleries and sports events she longed to attend. So far, she hadn't been to any of them.

Dan's hand rested lightly on the small of her back. His gesture gave her an unfamiliar sense of security. He was a real gentleman, she thought. How lucky for the woman in his life!

As they entered the small restaurant he commented, "Well, I suppose we should brace ourselves for the upcoming Minnesota winter." Becky knew she should respond with more small talk about the weather, the city, the job—anything. But she just couldn't. All she could do was murmur an agreement.

Dan located a booth by the window, then helped her slip her coat from her shoulders. His touch made her shiver.

"Cold?"

Becky shook her head. "Not really."

She slid into the booth and Dan leaned toward her. "What can I get for you?"

Reaching for her purse, she replied, "A hamburger and fries, I guess."

Dan's hand rested on hers. "Put your purse away. My treat."

"Oh, you don't have to—"

"I know," he interrupted. "I want to. All right?"

His smile was broad, reassuring, and it displayed two dimples she'd never noticed before. How she could have failed to notice *anything* about him was a mystery to her. It had been years since she'd been interested in a man. Six years ago, she'd vowed never to let a man get close to her again. And until now she'd succeeded. Until Dan.

She couldn't deny it any longer. He was handsome and kind, always willing to help. He had an easy manner and charm to spare. Everyone in the office wondered why he kept to himself. Maybe he was like her, she thought, just needing a little privacy. Whatever the reason, she understood. Sometimes it was just easier to be alone; that way, no one could hurt you.

His touch made her knees weaken, and she was glad she was sitting down. "All right," she quietly agreed.

His finger touched the tip of her nose. "Don't go away. I'll be right back."

Becky watched as he strolled confidently to the counter and placed their order, then paid for the meal, the waitress beaming happily all the while. No woman was immune!

Becky sighed and leaned back as she let the soft vinyl cushion her neck. She closed her eyes for a moment, feeling drained, exhausted. She'd kept herself busy with work, taking any overtime she could get—not only to avoid social pressures, but to make extra money. With her mother's arthritis worsening, Becky had to send more money to cover the needed medications.

Her father, a farmer, had died three years before, leaving no insurance money. Until his death, they hadn't known he'd not bothered to provide for his family. It hadn't been difficult to obtain health insurance for herself, but her mother was a different story. Her preexisting illnesses made her virtually uninsurable. So Becky was left with the outrageous medical bills that her mother's arthritis and asthma caused. She moved to the Twin Cities where her skills would be highly paid. Leaving her mother and the family farm hadn't been easy. She worried constantly about her mother living alone, but there was nothing she could do about it. Marge Thorpe had refused to move with her.

Becky didn't mind taking care of her mother financially. It was the least she could do. Her parents had always stood behind her, especially when her world had caved in. She owed them everything.

A few minutes later, Dan returned to the table and found her with her eyes closed. "Hey, are you falling asleep?" He grinned as Becky's eyes flew open and she sat up straighter.

She smoothed her hair unnecessarily. "Oh, sorry. I was just resting my eyes."

Dan placed the tray of food on the table before he slid into the seat opposite hers. "Staring at a computer screen all day is hard on the eyes."

"Mmm." Becky smiled as she took the hamburger from him. Then he handed her an order of fries, a large Coke and a cherry pie. "I don't think I'll be able to eat all this," she mumbled.

Dan had chosen the same meal for himself. He bit enthusiastically into a french fry. "I love these," he stated, before squirting a dollop of catsup on the plate. "Of course you'll be able to eat all this. It's been a long day, hasn't it?"

"That it has." Becky opened her cardboard box, revealing a double-decker hamburger smothered with tomatoes, lettuce and pickles. "It's been a long time since I've gone out for fast food."

He thought it must've been a while since Becky had done much of anything just for the fun of it, but he'd be a fool to say so. He watched as she took her first bite. But while the experience was obviously pleasant for her, it made him damned uncomfortable. The woman made eating a plain old hamburger a sensual experience. After all these years, he would have thought he was far too old for the kind of thoughts he was having. Why was it that in one short hour his self-imposed celibacy had suddenly become a burden? Sensual awareness of Becky Thorpe seemed to occupy his entire nervous system! True, he'd thought of her almost daily. Yet these had been only passing thoughts; brief fantasies he managed to keep under control. Until tonight. A

man couldn't dream forever; desire had finally caught up
with him.

Right now, she was swirling a fry in her own catsup,
looking like she was enjoying every minute of it. When was
the last time he'd seen anyone take such delight in simple
things? Back home in California, life had been complex and
fast-paced. Because of his father's success, Dan had had
everything a boy could want—the latest dirt bike, the flash-
iest sports car, anything he asked for. Then he'd grown up
and decided that life was more than the accumulation of
material wealth. Life meant taking delight in small things,
experiencing the moment, sharing with others. Tonight he
was watching a woman eating a hamburger with obvious
pleasure. It was wonderful.

"Looks like you're enjoying it," he commented, determined to keep things friendly and straightforward. If she
knew how her actions inflamed him, she'd take off running.

She nodded, touching the side of her mouth with her
napkin, and Dan silently cringed. Didn't she have any idea
how *appealing* she was?

She shrugged. "I never seem to have a chance to eat out."

He'd often noticed her in the company lunchroom, eating her sandwich from a brown sack as she read a library
book. Usually she sat alone; sometimes she was with her
friend Sarah. He'd also noticed that she avoided all the
company's social events.

"Then you're too busy," Dan ventured. "You need time
to go out, have fun."

"It can't be helped."

Dan frowned, dipping another fry into catsup. "What
can't be helped?"

"Oh, just work, that's all."

"You live alone, don't you?"

"That's right. How'd you know?"

Dan tried to appear nonchalant as he answered. "Oh, I
just assumed it."

"How about you? You live by yourself? What about your family?"

Dan knew she had changed the focus of their conversation to him. For now, he'd go along with it. "I live alone, too," he replied. "In a town house on Snelling."

Becky listened as he mentioned one of the main streets in town.

He went on, "My mother lives in Los Angeles."

She shook her head. "That's so far away. What brings you out here?"

Dan sighed, finishing his hamburger before he answered. "Just wanted to try things alone for a while." While his statement ended the topic, she was sure there was more to Dan than he'd said. Men just didn't pop out of nowhere these days—especially sophisticated men who wore obviously hand-tailored, expensive suits.

The rest of the meal passed with the usual light conversation. Becky was surprised to find herself relaxing; she even contributed her share of banter. They found that they both enjoyed listening to jazz and soft rock, liked Italian food and thought the Minnesota Twins had a good chance to win the World Series.

Becky couldn't remember when she'd had more fun.

"I'm stuffed," she said at last, picking up the cardboard box that held her pie. "And I haven't even had a bite of this."

Dan was just finishing his dessert. He looked up and grinned. "Take it home, then. A midnight snack."

Becky laughed, dropping it into her purse. "You talked me into it."

"Good." Dan didn't know why he felt so inordinately pleased that she'd enjoyed the cheap meal. He just knew that he did.

"Come on." He was on his feet, offering his hand to help her slide out of the booth.

She placed her small hand in his large one. The touch seemed magnetic, and they stared at each other for just a

minute. Becky was the first to look away, but Dan was the
first to speak. Holding out her coat, he said, "I'll walk you
to your car."

"I take the bus."

"You don't have a car?" Dan asked. How did she manage in a large city like this without a car?

Becky shook her head. "Never got around to getting
one." She looked at his expression and laughed. "It's not
that bad. The buses are convenient."

"Well, not tonight." Dan helped her put her coat on, his
fingers resting longer than necessary on her shoulders.
Slowly, and very gently, he put his hand under her hair,
lifting it over the collar of her coat before his hands
smoothed it back into place. Becky shivered. She was having a hard time remembering that he probably had several
women at his beck and call.

"It's perfectly safe." She managed to find her voice.

"Uh-uh, not tonight. I'm driving you home," he insisted.

"You don't—"

"Yes, I do." His face softened as he looked at her. "Now,
don't argue."

"But—"

He put his finger to her lips to silence her. Just his touch
was enough to jolt her into silence. She'd better give up before anything else happened. So she simply nodded.

"That's better." He ushered her out of the restaurant.
Walking quickly to the office parking lot, he helped her into
his black, midsize, luxury car. Getting into the driver's seat,
he reached over to fasten her seat belt. The closeness unnerved her, and she was glad the darkness hid her reaction.
The car hummed softly to life, and with one flick of his finger, quiet instrumental music flooded the air. Becky rev-
eled in the comfort. Except for a brief exchange about the
best route to her apartment, they were silent.

When they arrived at her building, Dan parked the car and began to unfasten his seat belt. Becky's hand on his arm stopped him. "I'll say good night here."

Dan shook his head. "I'll see you to your door."

"No." She inwardly cringed as she realized how clipped her answer sounded. But she couldn't help it. In some vague yet certain way, she sensed that allowing him into her building meant allowing him into her life. She couldn't risk it. Even after all this time, what Michael had done to her still festered. Although something told her Dan was different, and she wanted to trust him, she just couldn't. Not yet.

"Please, let's say good night here."

"No, I insist on walking you to the door."

Becky shook her head. "I'll be fine. It's not that late."

Dan gave up. Whatever her reasons for ending the evening out here, he had to honor her request. She was a private person, and he didn't want to rush things. Intruding in her life too quickly would only make her run in the opposite direction.

Fear. Looking at her right now, as the streetlight cast a warm glow over her features, Dan saw fear in her eyes. But why? Who or what had put that fear there?

He raised his hand to her cheek, gently stroking the smoothness of her skin. "All right," he whispered. "But I'm going to kiss you."

Becky started to draw away, but Dan had placed his left arm around her, resting it on her back as he coaxed her to him. "Don't be afraid. I'd never hurt you." His last words were spoken in a whisper, the warmth of his breath fanning her face. His right hand sneaked under her hair, cradling her neck, tilting her head toward him. "All right?" She thought she saw a faint smile, but she wasn't sure. Everything blurred as he bent closer, closer, until their mouths touched....

The feeling was like nothing Becky had ever experienced. When he said he was going to kiss her, she'd wanted to run—and run fast. But she didn't. She had to find out if she could be kissed by a truly decent person without the panic and fear she remembered so well.

His kiss was gentle, tender, soft and sensuous all at once. And she felt herself responding, matching his kiss with her own, giving back the tenderness he was giving her.

He stopped much too soon. Yet he seemed unhurried as his hand stroked the back of her neck. "Good night," he murmured before his lips touched her forehead, her nose, her cheek in little kisses that rained delight. "Say good night, Becky," Dan teased.

Becky looked up, her arms braced on his for support. "Good night. And . . . thank you."

"My pleasure," Dan returned. "I always enjoy feeding hungry, gorgeous women."

She blushed at the compliment, letting him believe that the meal was exactly what she was thanking him for. It wasn't. She was thanking him for that kiss, which had opened the window to her heart, just a little. It had been so long.

She hurried out of the car and waved. Dan made sure she was safely inside the building before he drove off.

Later, in bed, she realized they hadn't even mentioned the computer program she was supposed to learn that night.

Two

The next morning Becky awoke to the sound of a ringing telephone. Glancing at her alarm clock, she groaned. Almost time to get up. Sleepily she groped for the phone.

"Hello?"

"Good morning, darling," the soft voice replied.

"Mom." Becky sat up, smiling. "You sound good, Mom."

"Oh, I am, darling. You'll never guess what I've just done."

It wasn't unusual for Marge Thorpe to begin a new hobby or adventure. Her health problems slowed her down, but she kept trying new things. It was her mother's infectious zest for living that gave Becky the encouragement to go on after her disastrous love affair. If you could even call it a love affair.

"What are you trying now, Mom?" She cradled the receiver on her shoulder as she reached for her hairbrush.

"I pulled out that quilt we were working on last year. Do you remember it?"

"Sure I do," Becky returned. "It was that wedding-ring pattern. I'll never forget how hard we worked on that thing. It was way too ambitious a project for one week of vacation."

Marge chuckled. "We did work, didn't we? But I thought I'd finish it and enter it in the annual craft show. It's in a couple of weeks, you know."

"Already? I didn't realize how fast the time's going. Just don't work too hard, Mom, all right?" Becky was worried; her mother tended to overdo and then pay the price later. "Are you taking your medication faithfully?"

"Oh, Becky," her mother said, "you don't have to worry so much. Of course I'm taking the medicine, but I've never felt better."

"Good." Becky stood up. "I have to go, Mom. I need to get ready for work."

"It is that time, isn't it? I wouldn't have bothered you this morning, but I tried last night and you didn't answer."

"I was out, Mom."

"Obviously." Marge hesitated for a minute. "With your friend Sarah?"

"No, Mom, not Sarah."

"Darling, it wasn't a man, was it?"

Becky shut her eyes. She couldn't lie to her mother, but she knew what was coming. "Yes, it was."

"Oh, do be careful, Becky," her mother warned. "I don't want to see you hurt again."

"He won't hurt me, Mom."

"And how do you know that?"

Becky smiled, thinking about Dan. "He's nice. He's helped me at work so many times I feel I know him already."

Marge waited a minute, then said, "You haven't always been the best judge of character, dear. I don't mean to remind you, but..."

"I know, Mom. I really have to go. It's getting late."

"All right," Marge answered. "Be careful, you hear?"

"Yes, I will," Becky answered patiently. "I'll be looking forward to seeing that quilt."

"It'll be done soon," Marge predicted. "Perhaps you could come home for the craft show?"

Becky twisted the telephone cord. "I might just do that." She gave a small laugh. "Then I could check up on you."

Exasperated, her mother replied, "I'm not a child, Becky."

"Humor me, okay, Mom?"

"All right. I love you, Becky."

"Love you, too, Mom. G'Bye."

Becky hung up, then glanced at the time. She'd have to hurry. Punctuality was important to her; she'd never once been late for work.

"I'll see if I can restore the files." Dan finished speaking with the personnel manager just as his second line buzzed. Another call. He'd never finish if things were going to keep interrupting him. Thanks to his evening with Becky, his computer game—Daniel's Revenge—was still unfinished.

He thought for a minute, still holding the phone receiver against his ear. Not that last evening had been a washout. Far from it. Becky was delightful, in an unpretentious sort of way. He suspected that the clothes she wore were purposely selected to allow her to fade into the background. But it didn't work.

Dan smiled as he remembered how her suit clung to her petite frame, showing off her feminine curves. She was lovely, and he wanted to touch her, slowly and sweetly. He wanted to hold her.

And her taste. The little kiss last night had been wonderful. He felt his body respond accordingly as he imagined how it would be to make slow, tender love with her, to have her respond to him as a woman. He was curious to see just what was under those clothes. Would her lingerie be just as discreet and simple? Or outrageously feminine? Lace? Silk?

He cleared his throat and ran his finger under his collar. This was not the time to be daydreaming. He knew from company gossip that she hadn't dated anyone recently, but that didn't mean he was the right man for her. His life—his real life—was demanding, harried and public. Very public. In a few short months, he'd have to return to the family business in California. He found himself thinking about it often, dreading it. No, that wasn't the kind of life for a woman like Becky; he was more sure of that than ever. She valued her privacy too much. She hadn't even wanted him in her apartment building last night! So why was he suddenly thinking these crazy thoughts about big feather beds and white picket fences, about falling in love...and getting married? He hardly knew her! But he did know that she had nothing in common with who he really was.

She enjoyed the simple pleasures in life, like that hamburger last night. Once in California, Dan knew his meals were far more likely to be five-course lobster or steak dinners, eaten with business associates.

And then there was his mother. No, there were just too many obstacles.

He was struggling to keep his perspective. Their kiss last night had been just that—a warm, cozy kiss. Short and sweet. That was all it was for her. Just a kiss. And for him, too. Wasn't it?

He'd never allowed his mind to wander like this before. Determinedly he punched the button on his phone. "Dan Simmons here."

"It's me, darling," a pleasant voice crooned to him. Dan grimaced. He should have written sooner.

"Hello, Mother," he answered dutifully. "How are you?"

"I'm just fine, Daniel. But I miss you. And I haven't heard from you in a while, so I thought I'd do the motherly thing and check up on my one and only child."

"I'm sorry, Mom. I should have written or called."

"As long as you're all right."

Twisting a paper clip into a yet-to-be-defined shape, Dan listened to his mother. Audrey Simmons was one of a kind. Left alone when his dad died, she'd insisted that Dan continue with his own life and not worry about her. She'd encouraged him to leave California, to sow the proverbial wild oats. To experience a different kind of life—for a while. In time, he knew, she expected him back, running the com pany his father had worked long and hard to develop and make flourish. Both he and his mother wanted it to continue to flourish. They were beginning to branch out, marketing their gourmet coffees, teas and desserts in Europe and Canada. They didn't need him now, did they?

He began straightening the paper clip. "Mom, you worry too much. I'm fine. Uh, is everything going smoothly there?"

His mother chuckled before she replied. "Yes, of course. And a mother *is* entitled to worry." She paused briefly, then continued, "Daniel, I'd like to see you. We could have the jet at Minneapolis-St. Paul International in a few hours. How about it? There's a stockholders' party in—"

"No, Mother. Not now." Dan firmly interrupted his mother's plans. While he loved her dearly, and while he was willing, eventually, to assume company responsibilities, Dan didn't think he'd ever be able to live the highly social, highly visible life of a business tycoon.

As the only child of Audrey and Owen Simmons, it was taken for granted that he would step into his father's shoes, and become the company's CEO.

In a few years, he would, but right now he was enjoying his life in Minneapolis. He treasured his anonymity. For the past few years, he had succeeded in fooling the press. Absolutely no one had connected him with the Simmons empire, and he'd been free to continue his employment in the computer field unknown.

He stayed away from California, venturing there only at Christmas and on June twelfth, the day on which his baby sister had died twenty years earlier, of sudden infant death syndrome. Keeping to this strict schedule had been difficult, because he was aware how much his mother missed him. But for the first time in his life, Dan knew the freedom he'd always craved—the chance to do what he wanted, with no one's expectations to satisfy but his own. And he loved it.

"Mother, we've been through this before. The press follows you everywhere. They'll find out about me and that'll be the end of my life here. I don't mean to sound selfish, but I'm not ready to come back yet."

"Daniel Owen Simmons, what am I going to do with you?" His mother's voice rang out, clear and crisp.

"Mom, just be patient, please?" Dan leaned back in his chair, tossing the bent wire across his desk and into the trash.

"All right," Audrey replied, obviously resigned to the fact that she wouldn't be visiting him. "But this party is special. Frank Putnam is bringing his daughter, Alicia, and I wanted you to meet her. And what's the point of having a jet if you can't use it for your own purposes?"

Dan rolled his eyes and stifled a groan. "No, Mother. For Pete's sake, stay away from Minneapolis with that jet. I'd be forced to move on after that kind of publicity."

"Or move home."

"Not yet." Dan's voice was low. "I told you. I'll come back to Los Angeles when I'm ready."

"Daniel, really. Haven't you tired of Minneapolis by now? I want to see you."

"And see me married, I'm sure," Dan added.

Audrey chuckled. "Well, that too, of course. I'm not getting any younger dear, and I *would* like a grandchild or two."

Dan winced. This was the area in which he felt particularly guilty. He knew how desperately his mother wanted grandchildren. If she could have had more children of her own, he was certain he'd have several brothers or sisters. But it hadn't happened, and Audrey was content with Dan—as she'd assured him many times.

Dan wanted to fulfill his mother's wishes, all of them. But right now, he just couldn't. Especially not after last night...

It was practically through divine intervention that last night had gone so well. And he wanted more. He wanted to part those warm, welcoming lips of Becky's. He wanted to hold her, touch her, experience that softness he'd imagined so many times.

It would be wonderful to hear her laugh, to be able to chase that sadness from her face and replace it with joy.

But he had no right to hope for these things.

Because he couldn't tell Becky who he was, not now, when they'd only begun to know each other. Someone had already made her shy, fearful, afraid to trust. He didn't need to read her mind to know that she'd turn away from him the minute she learned he'd already deceived her.

Deceitful. Like it or not, that's what he was by not telling her the truth. He would tell her, though. Soon. Or so he promised himself.

He was not about to express his fears and doubts to his mother. On the one hand, he couldn't reject the very life his parents had worked so hard to give him. But he wasn't willing to give up his chance for a relationship with Becky, either.

"I'll see you soon, Mother."

"All right, Daniel," Audrey answered. "But I do miss you. I love you, you know."

Dan smiled. "I know, Mom. I'll talk to you later."

Before he pulled the phone away from his ear, his mother added, "Daniel?"

"Yes, Mom?"

"How much longer, do you think, before you come home for good?"

Dan sighed as he raked his fingers through his hair. "Probably in a few months, Mother."

"Good. I'll look forward to that. Goodbye, darling."

"'Bye, Mom." Dan hung up just as a wave of nausea flooded him. It was always like that. The thought of going home rattled him; he couldn't help it. It wasn't the work or the business decisions or even the social obligations; it was the public scrutiny. He no more wanted his private life scrutinized than he wanted root-canal work. But there was no use fighting it.

If only he could grab that brass ring before he left Minneapolis. Being a success in the business world wasn't enough. He'd finally found a woman who interested him, and he was determined to have some time with her.

After observing her these past months in the office, Dan knew that Becky was different from any woman he'd ever known. He'd watched her do little things for her coworkers. When one of them had a problem, Becky was there, cheering the person with a small plant or some freshly baked cookies. She'd been the one to decorate the office for Christmas. During her lunch hour, he'd noticed her reading, obviously absorbing every word.

It was plain to see that underneath her quiet exterior was a woman with a passion for living. And he wanted to be the one she smiled for, cared for. And he wanted to care for her. He'd worry about the complications later.

It was late in the afternoon when Becky found herself outside Dan's office. She traced the letters carved into the nameplate on the door: "Daniel O. Simmons, Manager, MIS." Such a common name. There must be thousands of people called Simmons. But there was only one as far as she was concerned. A most uncommon man.

A brief smile curved her lips as she thought of the night before. She'd always wanted to get to know him. For the first time since Michael, she really wanted a man to be interested in her. But with her limited experience, she suspected that was going to be difficult. She sighed. If only things had worked out differently for her... But none of that mattered now.

She knocked sharply.

"Come in." The voice was muffled, indistinct. Not sure she'd heard correctly, she knocked again.

"I said, come in!" The voice was clearer now, and Becky opened the door just in time to see Dan crawling out from under his desk. His six-foot frame looked comical emerging from the small space.

"Just fixing a loose connection to the terminal," he explained as he brushed off his dark blue slacks and jacket. The process pulled the fabric taut over some of his more intriguing body parts.

Becky's face turned rosy as she realized she'd been staring. One look at Dan and she knew he'd noticed. Well, it was too late. So she'd been looking, all right?

"Hi." Dan noticed how her black skirt outlined her shapely hips, then fell in soft folds. His eyes trailed upward as she walked toward him. She wore a lilac blouse underneath the black suit jacket. Her long blond hair was pulled back into a French braid with a few tendrils escaping. Small pearl earrings were her only jewelry. She looked lovely. He swallowed hard.

"Uh . . . did you need to see me, Becky?"

She glanced down at the manila folder in her hand. "About this."

"What about it?"

Becky gestured to a chair set against the wall. "May I?"

"Of course."

Settling herself in the blue upholstered chair, she placed the work in her lap, then folded her hands primly on top. Dan thought she looked like a schoolgirl ready for a lesson.

"May I see it?" he asked.

It was hard to keep her mind on business when he stood there, looking so handsome. "Oh—oh, yes, of course," she mumbled.

While Dan sorted through the papers, she noticed her surroundings. This was the first time she'd actually been inside his office. It was tastefully decorated in shades of blue and gray. From the carpeting to the draperies, everything was perfectly coordinated.

"I had a good time last night," Dan said casually.

"Me, too." Becky was at a loss for words. Why did that always happen around him? Were old memories always going to get in the way, making her uneasy around men? Around *him*? Since last night, Becky realized that she wanted her past to be just that—her past. She had used it as a shield long enough. She wanted to *feel* again, to know what it was like to be held, to be wanted. Last night had just intensified this need. Maybe Dan would understand about Michael... and the baby... and everything.

"Becky, did you hear me?" Dan waved his hand across her face to get her attention. "This is your proposal for the new color monitors on your floor. It looks fine to me."

"Good."

Dan smiled as he realized he'd been right. There *was* something between them. An attraction, a mutual interest. He briefly studied the folder, then passed it back to her. Their hands touched, and Becky was reminded of the kiss last night. So short, but so wonderful. She'd never felt as wonderful as she had last night.

It was happening again. Just being in the same room with Dan, noticing how he looked at her, she felt desirable, even beautiful.

He was obviously attracted to her, too, she thought. *And that's all there is to it. Just attraction.*

"Where were you?" He met her eyes. "You seemed a million miles away."

She shrugged. "A thousand maybe. Certainly not a million."

What could she say? That she'd been wondering how to tell him about her sordid past? She gave her head a slight shake. She couldn't risk it; it might ruin everything. She liked Dan. But this was more than sexual attraction, she had to admit. He was a genuinely nice person, one who really seemed to care about other people. Now that she knew he was interested in her and she was falling for him, common sense and past mistakes told her to be very careful. She'd believed she loved someone once, and all it had brought her was heartache. Becky couldn't forget. She mustn't.

Now what? Dan asked himself. Forget the whole thing? If he was smart, that was what he'd do. Stop it now before they went too far. Before he cared too much, loved too much.

and, ultimately, hurt too much. But he couldn't. Already his body was betraying him, his mind following close behind. Here was a woman he could be friends with and more, a woman he could fall in love with. Could he risk it? Should he? Lord help him, he wanted to. And he *would* find a way to chase the sadness from those round eyes of hers, dammit. He just prayed he didn't put more sadness there.

"I'm working on a new computer game," Dan said abruptly. "I'd, uh, like to get your reaction. If you're interested..."

Becky nodded, eyes shining.

"You would?"

"Sure. If you don't think it'll be too technical for me." Becky pushed a strand of hair behind her ear. Dan watched the movement, every part of his body stimulated by that small action. What would it feel like to run his own fingers through her hair?

"How about tonight?"

"Tonight?" She swallowed. "I—I don't know."

Dan watched her hesitancy and again saw that closed look in her eyes. There was a part of her she wasn't willing to share. "Why not?" he persisted. "In fact, I have the disk with me and I could show you after work."

"You mean here?"

"Sure. It's in my briefcase, in case I felt like working on it during lunch."

Becky laughed. "You certainly are dedicated to the project."

Dan chuckled. "Either that or obsessed with it." He arched an eyebrow. "How about it?"

"Sure."

"Good. Is around five-thirty all right?"

She glanced at her watch. "Perfect. It gives me enough time to tie up some loose ends at my desk."

"Do you like Chinese food?"

"I love it," she told him, "but I'm not too good with chopsticks."

Dan laughed. "Neither am I."

She enjoyed watching this man laugh. His laughter wa
full-bodied, uninhibited. Gone was the serious business
man; a playful, lighthearted man stood in his place. She wa
seeing a side of him that she'd never known existed.

She grinned. "Tonight, then."

He smiled back. "Strictly forks."

"See you then." She walked out of his office, unaware o
the appealing sexiness of her walk. But Dan wasn't.

Three

"Now, if you press 'escape,' you can go back one screen to check your position before going on."

Becky was only half listening. The game seemed interesting enough, but she was too conscious of the man sitting next to her. Since he was engrossed in his technology, she had the freedom to study him. He was tall, lean and lanky, with just the right amount of muscle, she decided. He'd removed his suit jacket and rolled up the sleeves of his light blue shirt. With his tie gone and the top two shirt buttons opened, Becky was treated to a glimpse of the light brown hair that curled underneath. It was downright tempting. But what could she do about it? The sad fact was that Becky Thorpe hadn't a clue how to seduce a man—or even if she should. Her time with Michael had been brief, limited to one experience when he'd seduced her on a night she'd drunk too much wine.

But things were different this time. She was falling in love with the man. She hadn't expected it to happen, hadn't even been thinking about it. She'd seen him every day, worked closely with him when computer problems arose, and this attraction had just developed, taking on a life of its own. Sneaking up on her. She hadn't been able to stop it, even though she'd done her best to ignore it. And then the other night when they'd had dinner together, she knew it was too late. She was halfway in love with Dan Simmons, and heaven help her, she wanted more than a professional relationship with him. She wanted a personal relationship.

And that meant a physical relationship. Now, with a sudden, frightening urgency, she wanted to seduce this man. Tonight, and every night for the rest of their lives. She was ready to try. To be open, warm and willing. But how? Oh, she knew all the corny lines. She watched movies. "Where have you been all my life?" "Isn't it warm in here?" "Why don't I slip into something more comfortable?" She was sure the last one could only be used if they were in *her* apartment, but the others didn't seem likely to work, either. If they were drinking something—say a vintage wine—she could accidentally spill it on him. Even then, she'd risk dumping some in the computer, and any idiot knew that wouldn't gain her any bonus points. She sighed audibly.

"Becky?" Dan turned toward her. "Are you listening?"

"What?" Becky nervously bit her lip.

The intercom buzzed before he could answer. Dan leaned behind the terminal to shut the computer off. "Never mind. I think that's our food."

Becky stood and smoothed her long skirt, and while he left the office she walked over to the grouping of chairs in the far end of his office. Noticing the glass end table between the two chairs, she smiled. A plant would look nice there, perhaps a golden pothos. Then there was that blank wall above his desk. The perfect place for a wildlife scene. Pheasants, maybe.

Her eyes fell on the bookcase and she walked closer. When she'd first entered Dan's office, she'd noticed his collection of books, ranging from computers to the latest psychology. Now, as she made a more careful study, she frowned. If she wasn't mistaken, the top shelf held some very expensive-looking leather-bound volumes. Classics, possibly first editions. Where did a computer manager get that kind of money?

But that wasn't the only thing. Around the office, the gossip was that Dan played a good game of golf. After the company tournament, people had talked about his expensive equipment. Somehow, that didn't fit Becky's picture of the dedicated, hardworking man with no time for anything but computers. He'd managed to raise everyone's curiosity, Becky's included.

"The food's here," Dan announced as he came back in.

Ignoring the questions crowding her mind, Becky looked up and smiled when Dan walked toward the desk, two white cartons and a brown paper sack in his hands.

"Let's eat! I'm starved." Dan motioned her over, and offered her one of the egg rolls. The chopsticks caught her eye.

He pointed to them. "We have to use these."

Becky frowned at him. "You're kidding, aren't you?"

"I'm not."

"You said forks," she reminded him.

Dan shrugged innocently. "I lied," he replied. "Come on. Let's try them."

He chuckled at her mock fury, realizing how much fun it was to spend an evening relaxing, enjoying life at a leisurely pace. Doing simple, ordinary things.

Glancing at Becky as she wielded the chopsticks made him realize that he wanted to share those everyday experiences with her. Maybe it was only a dream. If she learned the truth about him, she'd probably bolt. But right now, they had time and opportunity. He ignored the warning bells going off in his head and showed her the correct way to hold the chopsticks.

"There, see?" Becky said after a couple of minutes. "How am I doing?"

"Fine, just fine." Warmed by her lovely smile, Dan grasped a piece of chicken, smiling himself. Even the food tasted unusually good. Becky seemed as excited, as uncomplicated, as a kid. Were simple pleasures really the best? he mused. He'd always suspected it.... With his thoughts engrossing him, he clumsily dropped a water chestnut.

"I can't seem to do this tonight," he muttered.

She laughed. "You're the one who showed me."

Dan shrugged. He loved it when she laughed. Her smile was a delight, and he instinctively knew there'd been precious little happiness in her life recently. He was about to change all that. If he could. And if she let him.

Becky picked up a mushroom. "I see you're better with computers than Chinese cutlery."

Dan snorted. "Apparently. And here I thought I was such an expert."

They continued eating, the air between them alive with tension. When at last they both lowered their chopsticks, claiming they were full, they caught each other's gazes.

Neither moved for a moment. Then his heart kicked into overdrive as he watched her pick up her napkin, stand up and lean toward him to carefully wipe his chin. Unconsciously, she licked her lips, and his eyes followed the path of her tongue. He wanted Becky Thorpe. He wanted to kiss her senseless, tasting all the flavors and textures that were uniquely hers. He wanted to slowly open those little pearl buttons on her blouse and feel her smooth skin. But he didn't think he could stop there....

When desire was this strong, fears were forgotten. Dan grasped her wrist with his left hand and gently pulled her over and onto his lap. His eyes darkened with desire.

Wrapping his arm around her waist, he traced the outline of her lips with his finger. No words were needed as he felt his way along her throat, felt her pulse quicken. And then their eyes said the rest—just before their lips met in a long, demanding kiss. Brushing his mouth against hers, he urged her lips apart. Quickly, his tongue sought entrance into the softness of her mouth. Even as her tongue met his, Dan knew it wouldn't be enough.

"Becky?" The question lingered between them, giving her the opportunity to back out. Instead, she put her arm around him.

Dan swallowed. His heart was pounding, and his hands were shaking as he reached for the top button of her blouse. "All right?" he asked before releasing the button.

Becky felt the cool air on her skin, but it didn't matter. Dan's kisses were all-consuming, creating entirely new sensations. She'd never felt this way, had never felt so beautiful, so desired. Determinedly she pushed aside her fears. She didn't want to think tonight, only feel.

"Just fine," she whispered as she placed her hands on his shoulders to steady herself. She could smell his light woodsy scent. All her senses were on overload as his hands continued on the path he had set. One by one, the buttons gave way. Gently tugging the ends of her blouse out of her skirt, he parted the material.

As his eyes finally saw the lace that covered her breasts, he inhaled sharply. She wore a lace teddy. It was beautiful. *She* was beautiful. Slipping the blouse from her shoulders, he saw the smooth ivory skin and closed his eyes as he inhaled her fragrant scent. And then he was raining tiny kisses on her throat, her shoulders. Tentatively he dipped lower.

This was how it was supposed to feel. She knew, even though she'd never felt it before. She was warm, eager, needful. When Dan hesitated between her breasts, Becky felt herself arch, giving him silent permission to continue. She closed her eyes. She was lost in so many sensations she could no longer think. All she knew was that she didn't want it to stop.

Dan saw as her eyes closed and she threw her head back. He couldn't think of anything but this lovely woman on his lap. Would he be good enough? Would he excite her? He wanted things to be so good between them that, later when she knew the truth, there would be no decision. She wouldn't be *able* to leave!

Becky was urging him on and slowly he pulled the thin straps of the teddy from her shoulders, then gently drew it down, exposing her very skimpy white bra. Only this small bit of lace hid her from his view. He had to see her. The bra straps followed and Dan reached behind her to unfasten the clasp. His movements were smooth, flawless, as if he'd done this a hundred times before. Once she was revealed to him, Dan gasped and Becky lifted her head, watching him as he watched her.

"You're beautiful, Becky," he whispered. "I want to make you feel good."

"You do. Oh, you do!" Becky took a deep breath. "Um, I haven't done much of this before."

Dan studied her eyes for a minute. "You mean lovemaking?"

She nodded, brushing a wisp of his hair away from his face. "I don't make a habit of being alone with a man." She smiled. "Don't worry, though—it isn't my first time."

"Oh." If he'd been thinking straight, he would have pursued that conversation. But of course he wasn't and he didn't.

She held his hands as she guided them to her breasts. "Touch me, Dan, please."

"Oh, Becky," he moaned, as his hands stroked her breasts, between her breasts, softly kissing her as his thumbs rubbed over her nipples. They immediately tightened, and Dan felt himself respond to her.

But he suddenly knew there had to be more than this. More than just two people eagerly seeking relief and little else. He needed to be sure that she was committed to him, that she felt the same certainty he did. He would need that when he told her the truth. He wanted to make their lovemaking memorable. For Becky. For both of them. He wanted it to be a prelude to a life of loving....

"We have to stop," he whispered, drawing away. He couldn't really explain it, but he felt an instinctive need to protect what he recognized as her essential innocence.

"Why?" Becky's arms encircled his neck and she held him close.

"Oh, Becky," he groaned, "do you know what you're doing to me?"

"I hope so." She smiled as he looked up at her.

"It shouldn't be like this, not for us."

"Oh?" She arched an eyebrow. "How should it be?"

"Long and slow, the whole night. And the next night. And the nights after that." Dan took a deep breath as he sat up to slide her bra and teddy back into place. "Be sure, Becky. Because when you come to me again, it's going to be damned impossible to get away."

"I don't want to get away," she whispered.

"Think about it."

Becky nodded as she buttoned her blouse.

"It was a wonderful evening," Dan said as he helped her up, then stood, grasping her small hand in his. "Before you go..."

Once again, his mouth took possession of hers. The kiss was hard and unrelenting. Becky's knees weakened as she leaned into him, and he caught her, aligning their bodies.

Finally Dan groaned and pulled away. "Look what you do to me!" He took her hand in his, guiding it to where she would feel his arousal. "Feel. I want you."

"And I want you." Her words were whispered, breathless.

"Be sure, Becky, be sure," Dan repeated as he draped his arm around her shoulders. "I can't get enough of you."

They kissed again. This time, Dan forced himself away after only moments. "I've never really wanted to play for keeps before." His thumbs stroked her cheeks as he smiled. "Now I do."

Becky nodded.

Dan went on, his voice soft, the sound flowing over her, caressing her, "Because it's never happened before, not like this." He set her away from him before pushing his fingers through his hair. "Becky, there've been other women, but it was never...like it is with us."

She was surprised at his admission, but didn't say so. Instead, she grinned. "I'm glad, Dan."

"I feel *more* with you, *want* more with you. But if you'd rather not pursue this, tell me now, and I'll understand." As she shook her head, he hugged her and whispered in her ear, "I may never let you go, woman. Be very sure you're ready."

"Dan," she began as she placed her hands on either side of his face. "I'm new at this, too. There was only one man before, and it ended . . . badly."

Dan brought her hand to his mouth, kissing each finger in turn. "I'm sorry."

The words were so tender, spoken so sincerely, she felt tears burn behind her eyes. "Oh, Dan."

Dan growled and gave her a final kiss. "Let's go before it's too late."

She let him lead her out of the office.

"Can I give you a ride?"

"No," Becky answered. "I'll take the bus."

"I'd feel better if I drove you."

"All the same," she responded, "I'm perfectly capable of getting home safely."

"At least, let me get you a taxi."

"All right," she conceded.

After helping her into a cab, Dan paid the driver, then stared after the car as it pulled away, wondering if a girl from rural Minnesota could be happy in Los Angeles. He had to face it: California was another world. For one thing, L.A. was full of seekers and drifters, people who'd left their homes, their towns and families, behind. People who were striving for elusive goals—always wanting more. Whereas here, people seemed more content. Everyone had family ties. Parents and grandparents lived in nearby farming communities, like Becky's mother. Could Becky leave everyone, leave everything that was important to her? Could he ask her to do that? He was scared—scared of losing her, scared of making her unhappy, scared of his dishonesty. What was he going to do? Thrusting his hands into his pockets, he let out a string of curses. What on God's green earth was he going to do?

Four

Dan sat at his desk, critically considering his life. It had been five weeks since he'd shared that first hamburger with Becky. Five of the most wonderful weeks he'd ever had. They'd done so many things together.

When they discovered they both enjoyed reading, they'd scoured Minneapolis and St. Paul, seeking out every used-book store. Both of them found several treasures, but Becky'd been thrilled when Dan presented her with a lovely leather-bound copy of her favorite novel, *Jane Eyre*. She thought he was a mind reader until he admitted he'd seen her admire it.

They'd done other things, too. A long walk around the Nicollet Mall. A casual date that found them at the Walker Art Center. A leisurely stroll through a nearby park.

He picked up a paper clip and played with it as he sat daydreaming. They'd also had a not-so-leisurely day at the new Mall of America, systematically approaching the place to cover as much territory as possible in one day. They succeeded in getting sore feet. Dan grinned, remembering the way she'd laughed when he bought her that small stuffed bear.

He would have liked to spoil her, taking her to places she'd never seen. Like the Ordway. Or the Guthrie Theater. But she was adamant about not spending too much money, stating that they both had modest incomes and she really didn't need anything fancy, anyway. He didn't want to raise her suspicions, so he'd gone along with her.

He gazed at the plant she'd given him last week. It was small, but she assured him it would grow rapidly. She'd selected it especially for his office, taking into account that his window faced east.

He picked up a manila folder on his desk, then just as quickly, put it back down. He felt frustrated. He still hadn't told her the truth, and he had absolutely no idea how he was going to. He'd already waited too long.

But he couldn't help it. How was he going to tell her that money wasn't a problem for him? That he had more than he'd ever be able to spend? For that matter, how was he going to tell her *anything?* Who did he think he was, anyway, playing with Becky's future like this? What about *her* needs? What would she think when she learned the truth?

He'd really done it this time. The woman he wanted was within reach, but he was afraid that if she knew the truth, she would slip out of his grasp.

Dan frowned. Becky seemed afraid of something, too. What was she hiding? He'd already talked with her—about everything, including as much about his family as he'd dared, hoping she would share things about herself. And she had. But there was something still hidden away. She'd told him a lot about growing up on a farm and beginning high school. Then she'd skipped several years until she came to work in Roseville. What had happened during that time? He wanted her to tell him, but how could he ask, knowing the secrets he himself harbored?

He'd tried to ask her a few questions about her high-school graduation, but she'd shied away from that topic. Well, he'd grant her the privacy she wanted for now. But he'd find out eventually.

Dan vowed to go slowly, secure in the fact that whatever, whoever, had put the fear in her eyes, it wasn't him. She trusted him. He wasn't worthy of that trust, but it was there.

If Dan was anything, he was analytical, which was the reason he enjoyed computers so much. They were simple and predictable. Every morning, you turned them on and the same menu stared at you from the screen. You typed in some information and the needed response promptly appeared. If only women—or one certain woman—could be like that!

In a few short weeks, he'd fallen in love with Becky. While that was perhaps uncharacteristic of him, it was nonetheless true. He'd actually been attracted to her since his first day at the company. But what he felt now was so much more than that, although the attraction was—admittedly—pretty intense. She made him feel alive, gave him a sense of excitement.

With a sigh, he realized that if his mother had anything to say about it, he would shortly return to California and the life he'd inherited. He remembered how long and hard his father had worked. Every day was the same. After an early breakfast, his dad kissed his mother goodbye and then left for the office. They didn't see him again until eight or nine o'clock that night. Of course, his mother always understood, explaining to Dan when he was a boy that his father was a busy man, that he made important decisions. She assured Dan that both she and his father loved him.

Dan knew that was true, but it was difficult to always be explaining to your friends why your father wasn't at school meetings or important events. Even now, it hurt when he remembered the track award he'd won. His father hadn't been there to see him do it.

It would be the same way for his children. He wouldn't be able to prevent that. His time would be as scheduled as his father's. Which meant that his wife would be alone, trying to fill the hours. And, later, his kids... She'd be raising them virtually by herself. The way his mother had.

Of course, she'd have all the material things she ever needed or wanted. But for Becky, he sensed, that wasn't so terribly important. It was one of the things that drew him to her. She liked to be around the people she cared about—like her mother. She wouldn't be able to stand being so far away from her. And he figured she wouldn't take to the idea of selling the family home and asking her mother to move to California.

He squeezed his eyes shut, trying to stop the beginnings of a headache. He couldn't tell her his secrets yet, he decided. What he'd do was spend as much time with her as he could first. Maybe if she fell in love with him, she'd go to California with him. Maybe if he made her his—in every imaginable way—the choice would be easy. Maybe then, she wouldn't be able to leave him.

"You've been out with Dan Simmons, haven't you?"

Becky took a sip of the black coffee. "Sure." The one-word answer was enough; she didn't see any sense in denying the obvious.

Sarah put her bottle of mineral water down on the table they shared and leaned forward. "Tell me all about it, Becky," she whispered conspiratorially.

"About what?" Playing dumb would give her some added minutes to think, and Becky needed them. She had to be careful about what she said to Sarah. Even though the two were friends, Sarah tended to feed the rumor mill a bit too often.

Sarah rolled her eyes. "Give me a break, Becky. You know what I mean! *What's he like?* I just can't imagine DOS doing anything impulsive."

"DOS?" Becky arched an eyebrow at her friend.

"Yeah, Dan Simmons." Sarah leaned back. "We just found out his middle initial is O. So all together his initials are D.O.S. Pretty appropriate, don't you think? You know, DOS? Disk operating system—computers?"

Becky laughed. "Honestly, Sarah, pretty soon you'll be taking horoscopes seriously."

Sarah shook a finger at her friend. "Don't make fun of it. I'll have you know that according to your horoscope for the next month, your life's headed for a major upheaval."

Becky grinned. "What am I going to do—clean out my closets?"

"Very funny. I wouldn't be so quick to make fun if I were you. You know, everyone around here talks about him."

"I've never heard that much," Becky muttered.

"Of course not," Sarah responded, "you're always busy. But people are definitely interested in finding out more about Dan. He's great at his job, but ever since he was hired, he's pretty much kept to himself. It's almost as if he's . . . hiding something, you know?"

"That's ridiculous," Becky said firmly. "He's just like us—busy with work and struggling to make ends meet."

And yet . . . there were a few things that didn't add up. The expensive books, for instance. But maybe he'd inherited them—that was certainly possible. Becky brightened at the thought. "He isn't hiding anything," she insisted again.

"If you say so," Sarah muttered. "But he's been the main topic of conversation for months."

Becky finished her coffee and picked up her empty cup. "Well, I can tell you this much," she said. "He's fun to be with, smart and a real gentleman."

"So he didn't kiss you on the first date, right?" Sarah drew a deep breath. "Why am I not surprised?"

Becky put her hands in the side pockets of her midnight-blue ankle-length skirt. "I wouldn't say that."

"So he did kiss you? How was it?"

Becky frowned. "Honestly, Sarah, you don't think I'm going to tell you? It'd be all over the office in two minutes."

"Becky, this is Sarah, remember? I already know he's taken you to every bookstore within driving distance." She stood up, too, placing her water bottle in the appropriate recycling bin.

"You know that?" Becky said.

One look at Becky's stunned expression and Sarah began to stammer, "Well, uh, you know, Becky." She hesitated. "The grapevine."

Becky shook her head. "Great. That's just wonderful. I should have known that nothing's sacred around here."

"It's just talk, Becky. Don't let it bother you."

Becky looked at her friend. "You know it bothers me. Why can't people mind their own business?"

Sarah sighed. "Becky, we've had this conversation before. Not everyone keeps to themselves the way you do. And when someone as interesting as Dan Simmons joins the company, there's going to be talk."

"I suppose," Becky agreed. "But I don't have to like it."

"Then just ignore it."

"What else have you heard?"

Sarah hedged. "Nothing much."

"Yeah, right. You're not going to tell me, are you?"

"Becky, I'm shocked! We tell each other everything."

Becky glanced at the clock. "Break's over. We need to be getting back."

Shrugging, Sarah opened the door. "I suppose this means I'm not going to find out more about your budding romance."

"You've got that right," Becky said as they stood in the hallway.

"It's a shame," Sarah teased. "Just when it's really getting interesting, you clam up." Her tone grew more serious. "But people aren't going to stop talking until they satisfy their curiosity. And," she added with a twinkle, "I wouldn't mind learning a little more about DOS myself. In the interests of upgrading my computer skills, of course!"

Becky smiled weakly. "You're incorrigible, Sarah."

Her friend chuckled as she headed down the opposite hallway. "Maybe you're right."

Becky walked back to her office, lost in thought. What Sarah said was true—she *should* ignore the gossip. But she couldn't. She didn't like being the subject of speculation and rumor. And she couldn't help resenting the invasion of her privacy.

Shaking her head, Becky returned to her desk and the stack of reports she'd left only fifteen minutes ago. Two more hours and she could call it a day.

With her oversize Mickey Mouse nightshirt on and her feet in large woolly socks, Becky sank onto her sofa, exhausted. Not that the day had been particularly bad; work was never difficult. But she still felt bothered by the stares she'd endured. The office had never found her behavior all that interesting before! What she'd done—and what seemed to be everyone's business—was go out with Dan Simmons. Ever since he'd arrived on the scene, people had considered him something of an enigma. Now that she thought about it, he *did* seem awfully careful when he revealed anything about himself or his family, even to her. Why?

She scolded herself. Sarah's suspiciousness was beginning to infiltrate her thinking. She was going to have to stop that. He probably just wanted some privacy, that was all. Like her. He went through his day calmly and efficiently, keeping his mind on his work. Since his arrival, the computer system had run perfectly. She admired his dedication to the company.

Becky was not normally a courageous person. This time she'd surprised herself; she'd taken a risk. And it had worked out! All along, Becky had felt that Dan might be interested in her, and so, by some miracle, she'd found the courage to approach him, to respond to his overtures, to go out with him. It was the first time since Michael....

She covered her shapely legs with her old granny-square afghan and snuggled more deeply into the sofa. She closed her eyes, thinking how wonderful it was that Dan was interested in her. He was interested in *her!*

Dan slid his glasses from his face and pinched the bridge of his nose. He'd spent all day staring at a computer terminal and all evening reading at home. He was exhausted and his eyes burned.

Sitting in his favorite chair, he leaned back, stretching his tired muscles. He'd shed his tie right after work; now he unbuttoned a few buttons of his shirt and slipped off his shoes. Staring across the room, he frowned at his computer. The game was going to have to wait. He'd almost finished it, anyway.

Closing his eyes, he indulged in his favorite fantasy. It was about the two of them, Becky and him, lying side by side in his king-size bed. She excited him, unnerved him, urged him to give more, do more. And he did....

Dan imagined tracing the curves of her body, imagined them looking at each other with darkened eyes. Then, in his fantasy, he leaned forward, kissing her eyelids. Finally he whispered, "I love you, Becky," and his lips took possession of hers....

He loved her! It was the kind of love that lasted; he was sure of it. All he had to do was convince Becky she felt the same way.

His phone rang. Rubbing his eyes, he reached for the cordless phone that sat on the table next to him.

"Hello?"

"Dan, dear, I'm so glad I got you at home!"

Dan sighed. "Hello, Mother, what's up?"

She hesitated.

"Mom?" His voice grew anxious and he asked quickly, "Are you all right?"

"Oh, heavens, dear. Yes, of course. Don't worry."

"It's because I love you, Mom."

"I know, dear. I wanted to talk to you before you heard it on the news." She paused for a deep breath.

"Mom, what *is* it?"

"Dan, I'm married." She spoke softly.

Dan wasn't sure he'd heard her properly. No, he couldn't have. He chuckled. "Mom, what did you say?"

Her voice was stronger now. "I said, I'm married."

"I don't believe it!" Dan was out of his chair, grasping for something to make the news a reality. "You're not serious, are you?" He paced the floor. It had to be a joke.

Once the news was out, Audrey seemed to gain momentum. "Of course I'm serious, Daniel Owen Simmons. We flew to Vegas last night and ... did it. A few of the local reporters have already tried to contact us. We won't be able to keep it quiet for long."

"Vegas?" Dan's voice squeaked as he tried to absorb the news. "Vegas? That's so ... unlike you, Mother."

"I know, but—"

"Who is he?" Dan interrupted. "Who's the guy?" His foot tapped out a cadence. Had he really been away so long? He'd seen her a few months ago, and she hadn't said a word. Not one word.

"Dan, would you calm down?" his mother replied. "You always get excited when something unexpected happens. I knew you'd take it like this."

Dan clutched the phone. "We're not talking about me, Mother. We're talking about you. Now, I want to know. Who did you marry?"

"George Barrington."

"George Barrington?" Dan echoed. George Barrington had been his father's right-hand man, his associate, for years. On his father's death, George had become acting CEO, with all the responsibilities and privileges the job entailed.

When had the man found time to court his mother, for goodness' sake? Hell, why did his mother want to be courted by this guy in the first place? George Barrington was a *bore*. He was a businessman through and through, a man who couldn't be spontaneous or whimsical if his life depended on it. Dan suspected George had never done anything for mere pleasure. All his actions were tied to the food business, the stock market, the latest developments in the economy. Dan had always thought his father had found a man like himself when he chose George. Predictable, hardworking, methodical.

Well, he'd been wrong. Obviously George did have a few impulsive moments.

"Oh, Dan, dear, don't be so shocked. George is a wonderful man." In disbelief, Dan could almost see his mother smiling as she expounded on the man's attributes. "He's so much fun, Dan."

Dan managed to choke out a reply. "Fun? Old George?"

His mother continued, "He makes me laugh, Dan. I feel wonderful when I'm with him. I feel loved and I—"

"You loved Dad, Mother." Dan didn't know why he felt the need to remind her of this.

"Of course I loved your father. But he's gone, dear. I can't bring him back—and I can't stop living."

She had a point there. Okay, so he was getting used to the idea.

"Where *are* you two living, Mother?"

"In our home, Dan. It was just so much easier that way."

Dad's home—the home his father had designed for his mother. Another adjustment. "I guess congratulations are in order, right?" Dan's mother was silent for a long minute. "Mom?"

Audrey's voice quavered a bit. "Be happy for us, Dan. Please. I know you want to stay in Minneapolis for a while longer. I just wanted you to be aware that news of this might make the national networks."

Dan rolled his eyes. Great! Free publicity about the family again. "Oh, Mom, I am happy for you. You know me. I just have to get used to the idea."

"I know, dear. Oh, wait a minute."

Dan heard some mumbling in the background as the receiver changed hands. "Dan! Are you there?" The booming voice could belong to none other than George Barrington.

"Hello, George," Dan responded.

"When you get some time, come here for a visit, Dan. This is still your home."

Dan nodded wordlessly, but George required no answer to continue. "I hope you decide to return to work soon. We need you at the Simmons Corporation—you know that."

"Yes," Dan answered tightly.

"Selfishly, I have my own reasons for wanting you home," George went on. "Your mother and I are thinking of semiretirement. We'd like to travel, take an extended honeymoon." He paused for a minute. "Son, I love your mother. I hope you and I can be friends."

Dan nodded again. "We are, George. Always have been."

"Yes, yes, I know. But our marriage changes things. I'll make her happy, Dan."

"I know you will." Dan believed it. If George was anything, he was a man of his word.

"Dan, your mother sends her love. We need to be going now—there's a dinner party planned for us at The Place."

"Goodbye, then." Dan remembered the exclusive supper club George mentioned. Everything in their lives was the same—rich, exclusive, reserved—as it had always been. Everything Dan had been born into, everything he wasn't sure he wanted to be.

George hung up, breaking their connection. Dan sat down again. His mother was married. Well, what had he expected, anyway? She was an attractive woman, and in all honesty, he hadn't really expected her to live out the rest of her life alone. But George Barrington? Dan sighed. Here he sat, twenty-five years younger than his new stepfather, wondering how to guarantee a future with a certain woman, while the acting CEO of Simmons Corporation had just done it—and apparently revealed a few surprises about himself along the way. George Barrington, *fun?*

That information was the proverbial last straw. Dan slammed his arm on the arm of his chair. The noise seemed to reverberate through the room, taunting him. It was full speed ahead! If George Barrington could do it, so could he!

He was definitely going by instinct! And he'd have Becky if it was the last thing he ever did.

He glanced at his watch. Ten-thirty. Too late to call tonight.

He'd call her early tomorrow, Saturday, and convince her to spend the weekend with him. The entire weekend. Day and night. He'd make it wonderful, exciting, unforgettable. That way, the secrets he had wouldn't matter. Would they?

Five

The telephone was ringing. Becky opened one eye to stare at her alarm. Six o'clock. Who on earth was calling her at such an ungodly hour on a Saturday morning? She pulled the quilt up around her chin. She'd just ignore it, go back to sleep and wake around eleven, as she always did on Saturdays.

But the phone kept ringing. And ringing. Whoever it was certainly seemed persistent.

Frustrated, she threw back the covers, sighed and reached for the receiver.

"Hello?"

"Good morning!" the bright, wide-awake voice sang over the phone. "Hope I didn't wake you."

Becky sat up. "Wake me? Dan, do you know what time it is?"

The minute of silence seemed extraordinarily long. "Oh, I'm sorry." The apology was soft. "I did wake you."

But to Becky, the delight at hearing his voice made the time unimportant.

He paused, gathering his thoughts. "I thought we might spend the day together. You know, breakfast first, and then maybe the new museum on Larch Street. How about it?"

Becky's heart was racing. An entire day!

"Well?"

Becky swung her feet over the side of her bed, raking her free hand through her hair. "I'd like that."

"How soon can you be ready?" Dan asked. "An hour?"

She cringed when she looked in the mirror. Her hair stood out like a porcupine's quills and her complexion was washed out. She'd have to make some effort to look good in only an hour, but she could do it. "An hour's fine."

"Great. See you then."

Dan hung up the telephone, smiling to himself. Everything was going just fine.

Thoughtfully, he walked into his bathroom, slid the glass door open and started the shower. He stood under the spray, enjoying the water against his skin. While the shower was invigorating, it was a poor substitute for what he *really* wanted to feel.

Becky's skin, naked against his. Cool sheets. Hot responses. His senses were bombarded by his imagination. Tonight he'd know how it all felt with Becky, how it felt to give her pleasure and receive pleasure in return. He wanted to spend each and every night in her bed, making love with her.

And in a few years, he wanted her to have his baby. Feel her body growing with the life they'd created together.

He stepped out of the shower and briskly rubbed the thick towel over his skin. He didn't know if Becky wanted to have children—it wasn't something they'd even discussed—but his instincts told him she did.

Dan smoothed on his shaving cream, wondering for the thousandth time if she'd ever be able to live in a place like L.A. It couldn't be helped. As much as he would prefer to continue his life here in Minnesota, it wasn't possible. He had responsibilities, to his mother, to the company, to the employees and stockholders. *With privilege comes responsibility.* Those four words of his father's echoed in his mind over and over. Privilege. Responsibility. Would Becky understand?

He just didn't know. By the time she found out, however, she'd be so much in love with him that... Dan frowned at his reflection. He tried not to think of what he was planning. It bothered him; he knew he should've been honest with her right from the start. How could he explain his silence to her? She trusted him, and he'd violated that trust. *Would* she understand?

He wasn't going to tell her today, but he'd tell her soon. Very soon. This weekend was special; nothing was going to intrude on it.

Becky finished dressing ten minutes earlier than she'd expected. Wandering into her living room, she spotted her mother's letter on the end table. It had arrived on Thursday; Marge often wrote to save money on phone calls, and Becky was touched by her thoughtfulness. This latest letter was filled with information about the craft show. Her mother mentioned that she'd finished the quilt—it was gorgeous!—and would Becky be able to come home to see it win a ribbon next weekend? It'd be nice to be with her mom for a few days, and the craft show was always fun. Maybe Dan would like it. . . .

Becky knew she'd come a long way. Before meeting Dan, she'd never dreamed she'd want to invite a man anywhere, let alone her hometown. But it was so easy to be with Dan, and she felt ready to show him her childhood home, to have him meet her mother. She'd invite him today.

The morning and afternoon had been good. After a hearty breakfast of eggs, bacon and pancakes, they'd visited the new museum. Then they'd walked the skyway in Minneapolis, staring out at the city. They had held hands, laughed, joked.

After they'd eaten supper at a popular sandwich shop— Becky's choice—she'd invited him to her apartment. That was a small miracle in itself. She'd always been so guarded about her own place that Dan was humbled by the invitation. It showed she trusted him.

While she hung their jackets in the closet, he noticed all the little things in her home. There were tiny exquisite figurines of angels on a shelf behind the couch. A quilted wall hanging decorated one wall, while cross-stitch pictures hung on the others. Several patchwork pillows lined the couch. A bookcase held an eclectic assortment, from the complete works of Shakespeare to current romance paperbacks. And there were plants everywhere, cascading from shelves, suspended from the ceiling, lined up on the windowsills.

"Make yourself at home. I'll start some coffee."

"Sounds good," he replied, hunkering down to read the names of the CDs near her stereo. Then he examined the titles of her books, and finally he studied the framed photographs on one of the shelves. Family portraits mostly. Dan was moved by the obvious love in all three faces.

After satisfying his curiosity, he sat down on the couch. He wondered if she'd ever invited a man here before. He refused to think about how much she trusted him. When the time came, he'd make everything right.

"Here we are," Becky said cheerfully as she walked in with two steaming mugs. Dan unfolded his long frame from the small sofa and walked toward her. She watched him, a spark of excitement in her eyes.

"I was wondering," she began, handing him his coffee. "My mom just wrote me, asking if I'd be able to make it home next weekend for a local craft show. Would you like to come?"

Surprised, he looked at her. "Are you sure, Becky?"

She nodded. "Yes, if you want to. It may be boring for you, but..."

"I don't think it'd be boring at all. I'd love to come."

"You would?"

"Sure. When do we leave?"

"Does Friday evening sound okay? It only takes a few hours to reach Eaton on the freeway. I usually rent a car."

"I'll drive," he offered as he bent to set his mug on the low table. "I don't want coffee, Becky," Dan said quietly as he put his hands on her shoulders. His touch was light. Becky's breath came out in a short gasp.

"Are we changing the subject?"

"We are."

Her eyes focused on the design knitted into his sweater. All day, she had refused to acknowledge that their attraction to each other was growing. Now, in the quiet of her apartment, it was impossible to ignore. She looked up suddenly to meet his gaze and knew he felt it, too. It was powerful and exciting.

Refusing to analyze the situation, Dan watched her as he pulled her to him. He traced his thumb along her bottom lip. She was so beautiful; he had to have her. Now.

Becky placed her hands on his forearms and studied him in return. His face was handsome yet gentle, sensual yet kind. In a few short months, he had managed to make her forget her past. She felt wonderful, as if, in loving Dan, she'd purged herself of the tragic memories. And she did love him.

His fingers touched her hair. He enjoyed the feel of the silky strands. "Becky," he whispered, "you give me inspiration. I want so much when I'm with you. I feel so much." He lowered his mouth to hers. "Tell me you do, too." His last words were lost to her as their lips touched.

His kiss was sweet, undemanding, coaxing a response from her. And she gave it. When her mouth opened, Dan groaned, allowing his tongue to enter her moistness, searching and steadily increasing its demand. While his mouth worked its magic on hers, Dan drew her nearer.

He measured her response, her willingness to be with him. Suddenly kisses were not enough. With a low growl, he pulled her tightly to him so she could plainly feel his arousal.

"I want you, Becky. Now." He held her still, waiting for her answer.

Becky nodded. She'd never felt like this before. And that made her realize she hadn't loved Michael. She'd never trusted Michael with the implicit trust she experienced with Dan, this knowing he would never hurt her. Tonight, she wanted him. He was the man she loved.

Tonight, she was going to make a new start, become a whole person again.

Dan lightly planted kisses on her face before following the angle of her neck down to the hollow of her throat. "I don't care about anything except us. Right here. Right now." He paused. "Are you ready, Becky?"

"Yes," she whispered. And then she began to softly kiss his neck, her arms winding around his waist.

"I . . . I may be a failure in the sex department."

"No, you won't." Dan placed his hands on her shoulders. "And we're going to make love, not have sex."

The slightly veiled admission of love stopped her. "Dan, what did you say?"

"I said love, Becky. *I love you.*"

He smiled, watching her eyes light up with pleasure and confusion and excitement. "You love me?"

"Yes."

Tears shimmered in her eyes. "Oh, Dan, do you mean it? Do you really mean it?"

He chuckled, touching his finger to her nose. "Don't sound so surprised. You're a very lovable woman."

"I love you, too."

"Becky," he whispered, before wrapping his arms around her. "Just let me hold you for a minute."

She did while they both considered the seriousness of their declarations. She knew there was no turning back. She didn't want to.

Dan felt like singing. She loved him! Everything would work out. Life's problems seemed small compared to what he felt. Nothing would come between them; he was sure of it.

"Take off my sweater," he said.

She obeyed, and when it was off, she gazed at him, letting her hands rest on his shoulders. She stroked his arms. She wanted to stroke the thick hair that curled over his chest.

Dan acknowledged her unspoken desire. "Go ahead, touch me."

And she did. Her long nails grazed his skin as she drew her hands along his chest. The hair felt soft, and his heart quickened at her touch. He stopped her.

"My turn. I want this to last."

Her knees felt weak, her body responding to his hands. He pulled up her blue-and-white sweater and reached underneath. Becky gasped as his fingers touched her smooth skin, moving upward to stop at the soft underside of her lace-covered breasts. Dan bent to kiss her, again seeking entry into her mouth and receiving it. All the while, his hands moved, unfastening the front clasp of her bra. He broke off the kiss to pull her sweater over her head. It joined his on the floor.

He slipped her bra straps down, letting the underwear fall to the floor. Then he looked and his hands cupped her breasts. "You are so beautiful. You were made for me. Look."

Becky didn't look. Her eyes were closed, and as she clung to him for support, Dan's thumbs rubbed her rosy nipples, coaxing them into peaks. It seemed to her that her body was intent on only one purpose. The more he stroked her, the stronger her response. She felt warm and wet. She was helpless as he continued his assault.

He lifted her to him, his mouth closing over first one breast, then the other. "You're so sweet, so delicious."

With one fluid motion, he picked her up and walked behind the screen to her bed, gently placing her there. Wordlessly he unbuttoned her navy slacks. Her slacks, shoes and hosiery were quickly removed.

Becky watched him. She supposed she should be embarrassed, but she didn't stop to think about it. Dan was doing a fine job of making her feel beautiful, desired. Never had anything seemed so right to her.

And then her panties were gone. She lay there for him, as his eyes rested on the soft curls that hid her femininity. Silently he stood, shedding the remainder of his clothing.

He sank down beside her, his arm cradling her against him. His arousal was evident, his breath measured.

What followed next overwhelmed her senses so completely that she couldn't have formed a coherent thought if her life had depended on it. They touched each other, Dan leading the way. No part of her body was left unkissed, untouched, and then his hand came to rest at the juncture of her thighs. She tensed.

"Relax," he whispered.

Becky didn't hear him; his touch brought her to the brink of something she'd never known. Instinctively she grabbed at him, her nails scoring his back, and held him tight. She was lost in a web of overpowering sensations. Just before he reached the peak, he moved on top of her, spreading her legs as he entered her.

Intense desire needed intense release. And Becky found it.

Dan was with her every step of the way. His own release came seconds after hers and he sank deep within her, joining her as they rushed into the world of feelings, responses, sensations. And in that moment, their lives were forever altered.

Dan pulled her closer, delighting in the feel of her soft skin next to his. Dear Lord, what had he done? Amid the contentedness, he felt the prodding of guilt.

How was he going to tell her now? She thought she loved an ordinary working person, like herself. Someone who waited for each paycheck to keep him out of debt. How would she feel when she knew the truth?

Becky snuggled closer, a small smile on her sleeping face. had been so damned good! Today he'd made her his, they'd proved their love for each other, but once wasn't enough. . . .

There was just too much at stake. He loved her. He'd never been more sure of anything in his life. He sat up, watching her as she slept. So peaceful. So contented. And his. Forever. He'd never let her go. His love would be enough—it had to be!

And he'd make damn sure she didn't leave. How was he going to accomplish that? He had absolutely no idea. But he'd do it. He thought of how they'd spend their life together. She could quit work, follow her dreams. They'd make love every night. Warm and willing, she'd come to him and they would soar. Just like tonight.

Dan aligned his body with hers and bent to kiss her. He smiled as she stirred, her sleepy eyes opening to smile back. "Again?" she whispered.

Dan molded her breasts to his palms as he lost himself in their softness.

"Again," he whispered. Love replaced his troublesome thoughts.

Six

Becky opened her eyes to bright sunlight streaming through the bedroom window. Turning, she looked at the man beside her. The man she loved—the man she'd given herself to last night. It was better than anything she'd experienced or expected. They'd made love three times during the night, a night she wouldn't trade for a bucket of gold.

Smiling, she studied his face, admiring the angular cheekbones, the determined set of his chin. She needed to tell him she loved him, that he'd be her only lover for the rest of their lives.

He stretched his long frame, waking slowly. "Good morning." His voice was husky with sleep.

She'd never spent the entire night with a man before. But everything they'd felt and done together seemed so right. How could it not be?

"I love you," she whispered.

Dan propped himself up on his elbow, the sheet covering the lower portion of his body. He grinned. "And I love you."

Becky took a deep breath and sat up. "I didn't think I'd ever say it, not after Michael, but I do. I do love you."

Dan sat up behind her, his hands resting lightly on her shoulders. With one finger he traced her backbone, sending shivers of delight through her body.

"Do you want to tell me about him now?" he asked.

She rubbed her eyes. "I don't know if it's worth explaining."

Dan leaned forward and pressed a kiss to her bare shoulder. "I want to know everything about you, Becky. If it affected you, I want to know about it."

"It's really quite a short story." She moved to a half-sitting position and rearranged the sheet. "It went something like this," she began. "I was completely infatuated with him in high school. I thought it was love. He convinced me it was, so I...I gave myself to him in the back seat of his car."

Becky squeezed her eyes shut. She still felt humiliated by how gullible she'd been as an adolescent.

Dan smoothed the sheet over her breasts. His touch gave her strength and courage, and she went on, finishing rapidly. "I got pregnant, but the baby died when he was three days old. He was premature and his lungs were underdeveloped. And my mother never lets me forget about the colossal mistake of my life—because she doesn't want to see me hurt again."

Dan stared at her. She knew her eyes were too bright and it must be obvious that the memories still gave her a lot of pain. He kissed the nape of her neck, and his quiet understanding was almost more than she could bear. Struggling to hold back the tears, she shivered.

"I'll take it all away, Becky," he said, then gently kissed her lips. "We'll make new memories, a new baby. Marry me." His statements were punctuated by little kisses across her face.

"Marry you?" she whispered as the tears began to flow.

"Of course. How about it?"

Smiling through the tears that now streamed down her face, she threw her arms around his neck and pulled him closer, laughing and crying at the same time.

Dan chuckled. "I take it that's a yes?"

She nodded, still unable to speak.

"Good." He took a deep breath and eased her back on he mattress. Playfully growling, he cupped her breast in his and. A perfect fit. "Good. Because I want to spend the rest of my life with you."

And before she could respond, he was kissing her quite horoughly and provocatively.

They made love again. Dan refused to think about his secrets. Soon. He'd tell her soon.

"I'm hungry," Becky announced much later.

Dan arched his eyebrow, an amused expression on his ace. "You are? I wonder why."

Becky shrugged, playfully going along with his teasing. "I on't know."

"Could it be because neither one of us has had any susnance since last night, and it is now—" he looked at his atch "—nearly noon?"

"Could be."

"Well, then—" he gave her behind a little pat "—man 1d woman cannot live by love alone."

He stood in one fluid motion, unconcerned with his na-dness.

Stepping into his shorts and pants, he faced her. "Let's get essed and go out."

"Where?"

"The supermarket of course." He picked up his sweater d pulled it on. "We'll get some groceries and come back re. How would that be?"

She nodded. "I'd like that."

"Then what are we waiting for?"

It was Sunday afternoon so the mammoth supermarket, mplete with gourmet-food section, was crowded. Enter-
; the store, Dan felt a familiar twinge of guilt. These were e places that had made his father successful. Simmons oducts were everywhere.

Becky grabbed a shopping cart and wheeled it into th
store. He watched her as she looked over the bargains tha
greeted them by the entrance. She was sexy without bein
provocative, attractive without being glamorous.

Suddenly he panicked at the thought of telling her th
truth. Would she understand his reasons for not being hon
est in the first place? Would he lose her? He simply didn'
know—and he couldn't take that chance. Somehow he ha
to guarantee that she would remain his lover. And becom
his wife.

Becky noticed Dan's silence and chose to ignore it. He wa
probably only preoccupied with some computer idea; he wa
forever developing new programs at the office. That was i'
she decided. He *couldn't* be regretting the wonderful nigl
or his marriage proposal.

Becky shivered with pure excitement as she thought abou
it. Their lovemaking had exceeded all the romantic notior
and fantasies she'd ever had. Just remembering how h
hands had roamed her body made her tingle all ove
Shamelessly she admitted it to herself: she wanted to b
home—in bed—with the man she loved. The man who love
her.

"What do you feel like?" Dan's question startled her.

"I'm sorry, what?"

Dan grinned. "What do you feel like eating?"

Becky grinned back. "Oh, I don't know. I wasn't thinl
ing about food."

"Were you thinking about the same thing I was?"

His gaze warmed her as he let his eyes drift downwar
Her breasts peaked under his gaze, and she blushe
"Maybe," she teased. "But we do need to get some food,
she added in a determined voice.

"Well, I feel like a BLT," Dan suggested.

"BLT? Full of cholesterol," she replied.

Dan winked. "I know, but what a way to go."

"Okay," she agreed. "If we have BLTs, then we ma
sundaes for dessert."

"What about cholesterol?"

Becky shrugged dramatically. "I figure it this way. If we've already eaten the bacon, we might as well really clog up our arteries with ice cream. Besides, I love ice-cream sundaes."

"Okay. Here." Tossing a head of lettuce into the cart, Dan proceeded to pick out the best tomatoes.

A few aisles later, he asked, "What kind of ice cream?"

"Chocolate marshmallow, of course."

"Of course?"

Becky rolled her eyes. "I absolutely adore chocolate marsh—" The phrase was never finished as she squealed in delight. "Oh, we've got to have some."

When Dan turned to see what had caught Becky's attention, he gasped. He'd come face-to-face with his lies. "Topping?" Luckily Becky was so entranced in her selection, she didn't notice the catch in his voice.

"Which one?" She turned on her heel, a smile lighting up her face. "Chocolate fudge or marshmallow cream?"

Dan's heart constricted, and his voice lodged in his throat. The doubts resurfaced as he eyed the bottles in her hands. It was all he could do to pretend normalcy.

He gave a nonchalant shrug. "Whichever you prefer."

She shook her head. "No way. It's unAmerican to be so ambivalent about your ice-cream toppings—especially when it's *Simmons* ice-cream toppings."

Dan cringed.

"What's wrong? I didn't say a bad word or anything, did I?" she teased.

"No, of course not. Pick whichever one you want—I like them all." He had to get out of this aisle, away from the truth. Trying not to think about the fact that, in an hour or so, they'd be back at her apartment and he'd be forced to eat the stuff, he motioned for her to put the topping in the cart.

"I'll take them both," Becky decided. "You know, you just can't get enough of these gooey gourmet sauces."

Dan nodded absently.

Becky prattled on, oblivious to his discomfort. "I wonder what he was like," she murmured. By this time, they were at the checkout counter.

"Who?"

"Owen Simmons."

Dan swallowed hard. "Why would you want to know that?"

Becky shrugged as she put their purchases on the conveyor belt. "No special reason. I just thought that a man who knew how to make desserts like this must have been a lot of fun."

"Oh, right." Fun? Dan couldn't remember ever having "fun" with his father; the man lived and breathed business.

"You should be interested," she commented. Dan looked at her with false calm.

"Why?"

"You have the same last name."

Dan responded lightly. "Sweetheart, there are millions of Simmonses in the world."

"Oh, I know. I guess it's just that influential and powerful people have always intrigued me. I wouldn't like to be in their position, and I think the public is too obsessed with the rich and famous—but they *are* interesting."

They were in the parking lot when he answered, "Oh, really? Well, Ms. Curious, you can forget about them. Right now, you have only one person to think about. And that's me."

He grabbed her by the arm, gently pulling her closer. "Don't you forget it."

His mouth found hers, conquering her token resistance with a hungry kiss. It was the kind of kiss that lovers give each other—and Becky was immediately lost in the taste of him.

When her lips parted, his tongue swiftly took advantage, darting into her mouth. Surely and slowly he remembered the feel of her, the taste. Reluctantly he pulled away, ma saging her shoulders as he calmed himself. "This is definitely not the place."

Becky nodded. "Let's go home."

Dan growled playfully, then gave her a little pat before opening the car door. "I'll agree to that."

"Well, to quote the only Simmons *I* care about, 'What are we waiting for?'" Her eyes twinkled mischievously.

"Darned if I know," he replied before tossing the grocery bag into the trunk.

Intent on each other, neither noticed the man in the dark blue suit who sat in a black sedan across the parking lot. The man made a few notes, then picked up his cellular phone.

Dan and Becky drove away. John Riley didn't follow. He had gotten what he'd come for.

Seven

It was the day of the craft fair. The autumn air was crisp, the fall colors at their peak. Dan was pleased to be here with Becky. Looking at her in her blue jeans and pink pullover sweater, he had to admit she was in her element. Her eyes sparkled as she looked over each booth, stopping to share ideas or to lovingly touch the hand-stitching in a quilt.

They had stayed at the farmhouse the night before. True to his expectations, Marge Thorpe was a kind person whose hesitance about him sprung, he knew, from her tendency to be overprotective of her daughter. Knowing Becky's past, Dan understood it.

It was obvious Marge loved her daughter. Memories of Becky decorated the small house. As Marge had given Dan a tour of her home, he'd noticed photographs of Becky everywhere—Becky as a baby, taking her first steps, playing on a swing, graduating from high school.

"I couldn't bear to redecorate," Marge had explained. "She's my only child."

Becky's room still remained as she'd left it. It was all pink and white and feminine. Evidence of the girl becoming woman was everywhere—a baby doll sleeping in a tiny cradle, a baton leaning in a corner, pink ballet slippers dangling from a wall hook and a carefully preserved pink carnation corsage rested on the bureau.

"I've seen everything by now," Becky's voice was clear, a touch of wistfulness in it as she added, "I always enjoy these exhibits. If I lived closer, I'd show a few of my own projects."

Dan placed his arm around her shoulder. "You'd win every prize."

"Only if you were the judge," she returned. She thought for a minute before asking, "Want to see something else?"

"Sure," he replied. "Wait a second, okay?"

She watched as he selected a cross-stitched bookmark she'd admired. Quickly paying the exhibitor, he turned and gave it to her.

"You didn't have to buy me this," she said while she fingered the narrow ribbon in the design.

"I know."

"You don't need to spend your money on me. You may need it to develop your computer game."

Dan playfully kissed her nose with his finger before grasping her hand in his. "Don't worry about it."

"But—"

"But nothing. Now. What do you want to show me?"

"This way."

"Mom likes you," she said as they leisurely walked the two blocks to the little white church that sat on the corner of Spruce and Main.

"She's a nice woman," Dan commented.

"You know—" Becky hesitated "—ever since Michael, Mom has been so protective of me. But she told me last night that you're good for me. She's right."

"Thank heaven," he said. "Because I'm going to be around for a very long time."

They had reached the church. "I never come home without visiting Daddy," she explained as she led him to a small cemetery behind the church. Most of the graves were unadorned, but her father's simple gray tombstone was neatly trimmed with a small silk-flower arrangement. Surrounding his grave were four others decorated in the same way.

Dan watched as Becky knelt beside her father's. "The other graves are my two aunts and grandparents on Dad's side of the family."

Dan thought of his own father, realizing he'd never visited the cemetery after the funeral. The idea had never even occurred to him. He'd never felt close to his father because Owen had always been too busy for him. Watching Becky now, Dan was struck with a sense of guilt. Had he been too hard on his father?

"I'm sorry, honey," Dan mumbled, pushing his own feelings aside. He'd deal with them later.

"Don't be," she replied. "They lived happy lives. Dad was younger than the rest of them when he died, but he always said his life was full of rewards." She thought for a minute before continuing, "I wish I could have helped him more in the end. His medical bills were outrageous. He gave everything to me."

"All parents do that," Dan stated. He had never wanted for material things, but that was one thing his father had made sure of. No one would ever see a Simmons lacking for anything.

"I know," Becky answered. "Still..." Her voice faded and she bowed her head.

A few moments later, Becky stood, her eyes shiny with unshed tears. She gave Dan a tremulous smile.

"Come here." Dan reached for her and she buried her face in the loose weave of his maroon pullover. Soothingly he rubbed his hands up and down her back.

His loving ministrations released her tears, and he continued to hold her as she softly cried. Dan felt a little like a courageous knight—he was ready to slay dragons for her. If he could help it, nothing would hurt her again.

Finally the tears ended and she looked at him. He handed her his handkerchief, which she readily put to use. "It's just hard, you know?"

"I know," Dan agreed, even though he didn't, not really.

Wiping her nose, she said, "Let's go. I want to show you my high school."

"All right." He found he was eager to leave the cemetery and his uncomfortable feelings about his father. Had he just been too damned hard on the man? He didn't know, but he promised himself to ask his mother a few questions when he next saw her.

Becky gave him his handkerchief, which he stuffed into his pocket as they walked away hand in hand. Becky felt closer to Dan than ever. Being able to share this most private part of her life with him had been good.

Dan, however, felt differently. This weekend had proved what he thought all along. Becky was happy close to her family and the places she loved. Would they ever be able to work out a compromise?

He was certain of only one thing. How truly afraid he was to tell her the truth about himself....

One week after the craft show, Dan was sitting in Becky's apartment. They were sharing ice cream again. Ice cream with a Simmons topping. He managed to eat the stuff, but it seemed to stick in his throat, just like his deception.

He realized he needed her in his life. She'd become indispensable to his well-being, and he'd do anything to keep her with him. Anything. Right now, in fact, he was contemplating making her his legal wife before telling her the truth. Once she realized he'd lied, it would be too late. It seemed the only answer. She was the type of woman who wouldn't divorce him; she believed in love that lasted forever, like her parents'. Marge had spoken of her late husband frequently when they'd visited her. It was clear the couple had enjoyed a very special relationship. Becky wanted the same. Marriage seemed the only solution.

He wasn't proud of the plan. Far from it. But he was desperate.

Dan sighed. His father had drilled into him that most people were selfish and egocentric, interested only in their own gratification and that, if you wanted to make it in this life, you took the offensive, grabbing what you wanted, when you wanted it.

Dan didn't believe all that—never had. He enjoyed people, helping them, treating them fairly. In fact, his father used to say that his son had too many scruples.

He closed his eyes as the last spoonful of ice cream slid down his throat. He always treated people honestly. Always! Yet now, he'd managed to deceive the one person whose departure from his life would destroy him. And she would leave; he was sure of it—if he didn't do something soon.

"Marry me tomorrow." The quiet statement slipped out.

Becky looked up. "What did you say?"

"Well, maybe not tomorrow, but marry me as soon as we can arrange it." His voice was stronger now, full of determination.

"Dan, I...I mean—" Becky stood and walked to the window "—I want to get to know you better."

He set his dish down on the oblong coffee table and walked to her. He grasped her shoulders, then his hands found their way through her hair. His touch delighted her and she shuddered.

"You see?" His voice was a whisper in her ear as his finger lightly traced her spine. "We know everything that's important."

"Dan, I'm just not sure. This is all happening so fast. When I agreed to marry you, I figured we'd have a lot of time to do some planning. I need time to think."

But Dan was making it impossible to think. She closed her eyes as his hands found their way under her blouse, quickly unfastening the front closure of her bra. Pushing the lace away, his hands cupped her breasts, molding them. When his fingers traced over her nipples, teasing them erect, Becky sighed.

He was wonderful. He already knew all the ways to excite her. And she knew what kind of man he was. He was everything to her.

"Yes."

"Yes?" Dan echoed as he turned her toward him, quickly sliding her blouse off her shoulders. Slowly his fingers caught the straps of her bra, and it joined her blouse on the floor.

"Yes." Becky smiled up at him.

"Good." His answer was muffled as his mouth found the peak of one breast. Very soon the entire world reeled out of her sight, replaced by a kaleidoscope of feelings....

Eight

The next morning, Dan could barely contain himself. Becky had agreed to marry him as soon as it could be arranged! It would be wonderful. He'd be a good husband. Just thinking about her, her soft body and her passionate nature, was enough to send shafts of desire racing through him. With her by his side, he knew his life would be complete.

Trouble was he could not help feeling guilty about his decision to wait until after the wedding to tell her about himself. In fact, it almost doubled his deception. But was there any other way? The question rolled ceaselessly around in his mind.

He turned on his computer. Staring into the screen, his mind wandered over every word Becky had ever uttered about the rich and famous.

They'd been cuddling on her sofa the night before when a popular television program about the rich and famous had aired. She'd listened attentively, then said, "I wonder what it's like to own a company. So much money, so many decisions. I could never exist surrounded by that much power. It's too complicated."

He'd pursued the subject. "You've said that before. Why does it bother you so much?"

"I don't know. People like that are always on camera. The entire world is watching them, waiting for some juicy tidbit of information. It makes me angry that the public cares about such superficial things." She took a breath, then went on, "I mean, there are people out there doing really heroic things—like working on cures for cancer—but everyone only wants news about the rich. So, if you're one of them, your life would never be yours. I couldn't stand that."

"I'll bet they're used to it," he had muttered.

Becky had walked over to the television to change the station. "I guess. I couldn't. I can't even handle work sometimes, the way everyone likes to talk. Oh, look, here's my favorite show." She'd apparently forgotten her remarks, but he hadn't. And then when they were making the sundaes, she said, "Owen Simmons. Imagine. A guy who made a fortune on chocolate sauce. But then, the Simmons Corporation makes about a hundred different products, doesn't it? I wonder how wealthy he left his family when he died.... Oh, well. It really doesn't matter. Their life is light-years away from mine. His children probably went to fancy boarding schools and Ivy League colleges."

She turned to Dan and smiled lovingly. "I'm so glad you're like me—just a plain, hardworking person employed by an ordinary company."

He closed his eyes. He couldn't tell her. Not until she was married to him. Then he'd make up for it. Hell, he'd spend the rest of his life making up for it.

If Becky had stopped to analyze her decision to marry him right away, she would have been flabbergasted at her sudden agreement. But she hadn't. Not for one second. She was completely in love. She slipped the bottle of clear nail polish out of her top desk drawer. Not even a run in her new panty hose fazed her today. Dan was wonderful to her, in every imaginable way. She dabbed her hose with the polish as she remembered their lovemaking.

She turned on her computer. Work was the last thing on her mind, but it couldn't wait. She'd have to discipline herself. If she didn't regain some control, she'd be fired before she was even married. And she couldn't afford that. Now

that she was getting married, she wanted to save all she
could so they could eventually buy their first home. It would
be wonderful: saving together, finding just the right house;
then moving in and starting a family. Thank goodness they
both had decent jobs. She was fortunate to have her sav-
ings account. She already had enough money for a nice
wedding. Not a big, ostentatious one, but enough for a
modest party. And surely Dan could wait a *little* longer to
give her some time to send out invitations and hire a hall....
Positioning her hands on the keyboard, she grinned. Life
was good.

Audrey Simmons sat in her living room, her expression
intent as she listened to the voice on the other end of the
telephone line.

"He's involved with a young woman, Audrey." John
Riley, an old friend of the family, was saying. Audrey
should have felt guilty about having John, one of the best
private detectives on the West Coast, follow her son, but she
didn't. Not one bit.

Dan was her son, her only child, and she loved him im-
mensely. She wanted nothing more than his happiness.

As difficult as it was, she'd accepted the fact that he
needed to experience normal life. Being a Simmons was like
being a Kennedy—only on a smaller scale. She'd gotten used
to it. But Dan never had. Thinking back to his childhood,
Audrey remembered the times he cried when his birthday
party turned into a photo session for some newspaper. Or
that time she'd taken him to Disneyland and they'd been
pursued by a photographer for some tabloid.

So, she'd let him go. But that was three years ago, and
now the company needed him. *She* needed him. She wanted
her new husband to retire. This time, she didn't want to
share her husband with the company. If she could just mo-
tivate her son to come home.

"What's she like, John?" Audrey interrupted after a few moments of listening to him recite the woman's name, address and job title.

"She seems nice," John replied. "Good-looking in a sort of cute way. She's unsophisticated, a real down-to-earth kind of woman."

"And her parents?"

John paused for a moment, leafing through some of his papers. "Ah, here it is. There's just her mother left. They were farmers, Audrey. Dairy farmers in southeastern Minnesota, to be exact. Becky is the only child."

Audrey thought for a minute. "Dan and this Becky—are they serious?"

John cleared his throat. "They're clearly in love if their performance in the parking lot is any indication."

Audrey smiled. Young love. She was glad Dan had finally found it. He needed someone, and if this girl made him happy, then so be it.

"Do you think he told her about the company?"

John hesitated for a minute. "I don't think so. They eat out in burger joints and buy food in discount stores. Obviously he's not revealing that he's got money. Seems to be enjoying his anonymity too much to make a change."

"I was afraid of that."

"It's going to be a problem, all right," John agreed.

"Then I'll just have to fix it," Audrey stated in her familiar determined tone. When things were important to her, she possessed tunnel vision. And Dan's happiness was very important indeed.

John chuckled. "I knew you'd say that."

"You know me too well, John."

"Anything you want me to do?"

"No. I think I'll handle it from here," she said. "Thank you. You did a great job."

"Any time, Audrey. Any time."

After the line was disconnected, Audrey's brow knitted in thought. Then she reached for the phone again and dialed the number of the company's aviation service.

Dan knew he had to move fast. Disgusted, he threw the Simmons Corporation business report from Los Angeles onto his desk. Lord, how he wanted more time! But time had just run out. They were expanding so rapidly he was needed. It was too much for George and the two vice presidents to handle. Besides, George wanted to retire, and Dan couldn't blame him.

Dan leaned back in his swivel chair, staring at the buildings that made up the Minneapolis skyline. He'd miss this city. He'd grown to love it; it was clean, fresh, full of vigor.

As his eyes focused on the horizon, his thoughts turned to his father.

"Dad, how come you like to make ice-cream stuff?" he remembered asking him—among a thousand other questions his father never seemed to get tired of answering, Dan realized now.

"Because I knew there'd be boys like you who'd love to eat ice cream, Danny," his father had replied, affectionately pulling the front curl on his son's head.

"You mean you made it because of me?"

"I sure did, son. Because of you and your mother."

Until now, that incident was one of the few good memories he had of his father. He'd done a lot of soul-searching since that day in the cemetery with Becky. In his own way, his father had loved him. That's why he'd been so determined to make his company successful. While Dan would have preferred to have his father at home, he was beginning to understand just what had motivated Owen Simmons—the love of a good woman and the son she gave him.

Now that Dan loved Becky, the past was not as painful. Dan wanted to preserve that company and provide for Becky, too. He knew he was sounding a lot like his father but he would be careful not to spend his entire life focused on business. He'd have a family, too. He'd run the company differently than his father did. Not better—just differently. He'd delegate authority whenever he could.

He made his decision. He would return to Los Angeles as soon as he made Becky his wife.

Reaching for the phone, he punched in a series of numbers. "American Airlines? Yes, I'd like to know about your departing flights to..."

Becky's eyes were round, the sparkle of excitement in them dazzling. Or was it anger?

"Las Vegas!" she exclaimed. "Are you crazy?"

Dan had expected a number of reactions to the plan. But he hadn't expected this. "No, I'm not."

He looked around her apartment, glancing at the mementos that decorated the room. A tiny, ceramic, black-and-white cow sat on an end table next to a framed photograph of Becky and her parents. He picked it up and studied it.

"I'll go get some coffee," Becky muttered as she headed toward the kitchen. Coffee was the last thing on her mind, but she needed some space.

The photograph reminded him that Becky was the type of woman who'd want a nice wedding. She'd want to share that day with her mother in her hometown. Did he have the right to try to talk her into a fast Las Vegas wedding? And why? Because, dammit, he was too afraid to tell her the truth before he had his ring on her finger. He couldn't lose her, and at the same time, he couldn't deny that time was at a premium. He was, in short, caught between a rock and a hard place.

Becky returned with a small tray of Wedgwood blue mugs and a plate of homemade chocolate-chip cookies, which she set down on the coffee table. He stared at the cookies. They seemed to confirm it all—she was a country girl who wanted a simple life with the man she loved.

Could he make her happy? He had to try. Today he'd tell her everything—just as soon as he made love to her.

His desire had been building all day, and when he reached out and began to stroke her face, her slender neck, her breasts, he knew hers had been building equally....

"Let's have some ice cream to go with those cookies we didn't get around to eating," Becky announced later, swinging her legs off the bed.

Dan groaned. "Please, have a heart!" He was spent from their lovemaking, completely satisfied and more than willing to simply lounge around her apartment.

He smiled as he propped up his head on his elbow.

"Oh, come on," she insisted as she hastily pulled on a pair of pink sweatpants and a pink sweatshirt—minus anything underneath; a fact which Dan didn't fail to notice.

While he was relaxed and tired, she seemed rejuvenated by their intimacy, ready to conquer any obstacle.

"Let's get going," she teased, before playfully throwing his slacks at him. "I want to eat and watch the news."

Dan arched an eyebrow. "In that order?"

Becky smiled. "More or less." She sailed out of the bedroom, headed for the kitchen.

Dan's emotions were a mixture of euphoria and despair. Before his eyes, Becky had been transformed into a loving woman. She was sensual, funny, vibrant. While it was obvious she had a mind of her own, he couldn't help but be proud that he added a new dimension to her life.

Dan stretched before standing up, then pulled on his slacks, leaving the top button open. He made his way into the living room.

She watched as he turned on the television. His muscles flexed with every move, leaving her mouth dry. Yes, she loved him as a person, but she also adored him as a man.

"What are you grinning about?"

Becky shrugged, handed him a dish of ice cream and curled up beside him. "Oh, I don't know," she replied.

"Yes, you do. Now tell me—what is it?" He tapped his foot, then declared, "I'll just have to tickle it out of you."

Promptly he took both their dishes and placed them on the coffee table. Then he proceeded to do just that. Amid her giggles, he slipped his hand under her shirt and covered her breasts, delighting in the way the tips peaked as she responded to him.

"Dan, please," she murmured, breathless.

"Please what?" His hands cupped her breasts. "Touch you?" His thumbs gently teased her. "Kiss you?" The question ended on a sigh, just before his mouth touched hers.

Becky poked him in the ribs. "Oh, stop," she begged as she struggled to sit up. "Here's the news. I'd like to see if they mention the political caucus next week."

"I had no idea you were interested in politics," Dan said.

She shook her finger at him. "There's a lot you don't know about me."

He arched an eyebrow. "Oh?"

She nodded. "That's right."

Dan sighed as he turned up the volume on the television. "I'll have to remember that."

But Becky wasn't listening to him any longer. Her eyes suddenly became glued to the television set, her brows furrowed with concern. "Listen. Look at that plane. It's just like I said before. The rich can't do anything without someone watching their every move."

Dan watched in horror as his mother's plane landed—moments before she emerged from the aircraft with George Barrington at her side. He took a deep breath and swallowed, listening to the drone of the newscaster, " . . . departing now from the plane are Mr. and Mrs. George Barrington, primary stockholders in the Simmons Corporation, a firm known nationwide for its many products. Rumor has it that Mrs. Barrington has come to Minneapolis on business, but plans to visit her son, who's been living here for the past few years. . . ."

Becky turned slowly and looked at Dan. His eyes told her everything she needed to know. Her face was pale, strained, and as she turned to him, he could see the sparkle of unshed tears in her eyes.

"Now I know what the O. in your name stands for, don't I?" Her question was quiet but forceful. "You're Owen Simmons's son, aren't you?"

What could he say? What words were the right ones? How do you explain the long-term lie you've lived to the woman you love? Why did he mess around with the one person who had become his entire life?

"Answer me, dammit!" She stood, a questioning look in her eyes. She wanted him to deny it, he knew that.

"Yes. I am." There was nothing else he could say.

Becky nodded as she walked to her window and looked out. The silence seemed to echo in the apartment.

"Say something, love, anything," Dan pleaded.

Whirling on her heel to face him, she pointed a finger at him. "Don't you ever, ever, call me 'love' again. All those jokes around the office, nicknaming you DOS. Not once did anyone put you together with one of the biggest companies in the country. Not once!" Becky was almost yelling, on the verge of hysteria.

"Becky, don't—" He stepped toward her, desperately wanting to hold her, comfort her, explain to her.

"Stay away from me, do you understand? I never want you to touch me again!"

"Don't, Becky, please," Dan begged, tears welling up in his own eyes. "I love you." It was the only defense he had.

Becky laughed—a short, bitter laugh. "Love. You don't even know the meaning of the word! What was I, anyway? A little fling with some common Minnesota farm girl before you hightailed it back to Los Angeles and your corporate way of life?"

"No, never."

Becky silenced him by holding up her hand. "Well, excuse me, Daniel *Owen* Simmons," she continued, "I don't buy it, not for one second. You can have any woman you want, so please don't think I'm foolish enough to believe you've fallen head over heels in love with me, all right?"

Dan shrugged helplessly. "It's true."

She pointed a shaking finger at the door. "Get out of here, now! Get out!"

Her voice was a mix of grief, anger and betrayal. He knew there was no point trying to convince her in this state.

"I'll be back," he promised, before scooping up his jacket and heading toward the door.

"Don't bother. You won't be welcome." Becky followed him. "Go back to your mother, your company, the women who run in your own circles. And never come back here. *Never.*"

Her last words were punctuated with the slam of the door. Dan pulled on his jacket and slowly walked out of the building into the rich light of the setting sun. But he didn't notice the beauty of it all. Without her, there was no beauty.

Nine

It had been six weeks. Six long, boring, miserable weeks. Six weeks without Becky.

Dan paced the floor of his plush Los Angeles office. He had done the honorable thing. After handing in his resignation in Minneapolis and making repeated futile attempts to explain things to Becky, he had returned to the company that was waiting for him in California.

Why hadn't he played it straight? Because he'd been afraid he would lose her. But in the end, he had lost her, anyway. What was the use? His fate had been sealed from the moment of his birth. He was one of the privileged, the damned elite, a man without choices. A man whose wealth and status dictated his life.

Dan shut his eyes, pinching the bridge of his nose. He had to deal with his pain, realize he'd never get her back. But all he could think of were dishes of ice cream, slow kisses and long nights in her arms.

Becky felt numb all the time now. She pressed the appropriate key to return her computer to DOS, then mechanically went through the motions of cleaning up her desk, grabbing her coat, slinging her purse over her shoulder. She had ceased to live; she only existed.

She glanced at her calendar unnecessarily. She knew what day it was. It was six weeks and one day since the night she'd sent him away. And even though it had been the right thing to do, she couldn't forget him. Smiling sadly, she realized how important he had become to her.

She had found a man she thought she could live with forever, and it had been wonderful. Short, but wonderful. Ruefully she shook her head. Some judge of character she was! The man had lied about everything, and she'd bought it, hook, line and sinker. What a fool she was!

She slammed her desk drawer shut and walked out of her office. If only she could forget his passion, his warmth, his kisses, things would be a lot easier.

Looking around, she saw that the office was deserted. It was long past closing time. She'd worked late again, as she often did now. She couldn't bear to be at home all alone with her memories.

A rhythmic clicking of high heels startled her. She turned and found herself face-to-face with an attractive older woman. The woman was smiling at her, and even though Becky had never met her, she'd recognize that face anywhere. The news media hadn't done her justice. It was Audrey Simmons Barrington, Dan's mother. Becky's mouth went dry.

"Hello, Becky."

Becky swallowed. "Mrs. Barrington." She clasped her hands together and forced the words out. Why had she come? It was much too late for anything now.

Audrey smiled graciously. "Please, dear, relax. And call me Audrey. Can we go somewhere to talk?"

Becky nodded, leading Audrey back into her office. She indicated a chair on the right side of her desk. "Have a seat, please."

"Thank you." Audrey settled comfortably in the chair, crossing her legs and casually dangling one of the burgundy leather heels she wore. Her suit was off-white, elegant yet understated. The burgundy earrings, bracelet and handbag matched her shoes perfectly. Becky took in her appearance and silently admitted to herself that the woman hardly looked old enough to have a son Dan's age.

"If Dan—"

Becky's words were interrupted. "Before you say anything, Becky, let me say what I came here to say, all right? Then you can argue with me all you want."

"All right." The agreement was easy enough; Dan's mother couldn't possibly say anything that would change her mind.

Audrey took a deep breath, gathering her thoughts before speaking. "Before you get the wrong idea, Dan did not send me here and he'll probably have a fit when he finds out what I'm doing."

Becky looked up, surprised.

Audrey smiled. "Yes, I will tell him, Becky. I believe in complete honesty with my son. And now, I'm going to be honest with you."

The story began. Becky listened attentively while Audrey mapped out a sketchy profile of her life with her husband. They had met early in their college days, each one of them the typical financially strapped student.

Becky couldn't help but be interested when Audrey spoke of her love for her first husband, how he had worked endlessly to build a business that would give his family a comfortable life.

But Dan's father hadn't just been successful. He had been outstanding, building a financial empire in ten short years. Ten years during which Dan had been growing up.

Becky felt like crying when Audrey, tears welling up in her eyes, spoke of the daughter she had lost in infancy.

And then she spoke of Dan. Her dreams for him, her aspirations.

"But there's only one thing I really want for Dan," Audrey continued, "I want him to be happy, married to whomever he chooses, and I will welcome her with open arms. I will finally have the daughter I've wanted so badly."

Becky was speechless.

Audrey paused. "The woman he wants, my dear, is you. Oh—" she waved a hand in the air "—he has spoken so highly of you, your ambition and your goals. He's afraid he wouldn't be able to spend much time with a wife and she'd feel cheated or lonely. I suppose that comes from growing up with a father who was seldom at home. But there is one thing that happens to him when he mentions your name that has convinced me he truly loves you."

Becky blinked. "What's that?"

"It's his eyes. They sparkle when he speaks of you. He's just like his father that way—everything he feels is mirrored in his eyes."

"It wouldn't work," Becky answered miserably.

"What wouldn't work?"

"His life is so different from mine," she stated. "I can't handle it when people talk about me. How would I handle the media?"

Audrey gave an indelicate snort. "That's hardly an excuse. You wouldn't have to. That's why we employ people to deal with it."

"But—"

The older woman held up her hand. "He's spoken so much about you I feel as if I know you. You and Dan have so many things in common—a love of books, music, the simple pleasures in life. You both want a family. You love each other. He can deny all these things, but I know him. But for some reason, he's rationalized too much. He thinks he has to live in California, near the company's headquarters. But that's not true. The company is so large we have offices located throughout the country. He can choose the one he wants to for his headquarters. And that's fine with me. Now that I've met you, I can see why he loves you."

Becky's eyes widened as she listened to Audrey enumerate the obstacles and then overcome them. "Do you really think so? We could live anywhere? You know, my mother has asthma—she has to live where there's fresh air and minimal pollution." Becky thought for a minute. "I couldn't leave her."

Audrey studied her future daughter-in-law. "No, of course you couldn't. But again, that's simply no problem. As I've said to Dan many times, we have that jet, as well as several other means of transportation. The company only limits us if we allow it to. Besides—" she paused "—Dan and I have talked since he's been home. He's finally beginning to understand that his father really loved him. Dan has choices to make, my dear. He loves you, and if he thinks for one minute that you could forgive him, he'll make your marriage work."

"Oh, Mrs.—Audrey, I don't know. Do you really think everything could be worked out?"

"Of course," Audrey said decisively. "All you have to do is go to him. He's tried several times to reach you."

"Yes, I know."

"He respects your wishes," Audrey continued. "He'll leave you alone. So it's up to you."

Becky nodded, already planning a trip to California.

Audrey stood and extended her hand to Becky. "I need to be going, my dear. But, please, think about everything I've said."

"I will," Becky replied, clasping Audrey's hand warmly.

"Good. Then I know I'll see you soon. Let me know when I can begin planning the wedding. I love weddings."

And before Becky could respond, she was gone. Becky grabbed her coat and left the office. Why did she feel as if she'd just had a visit from her fairy godmother?

The day after Audrey's visit, Becky was working, her ticket for California waiting to be picked up at the travel agency. It was nearly impossible to keep her mind on her job when the rest of her life was about to be decided. As soon as she saw Dan, she'd know if they had a chance.

Letting her fingers rest on her keyboard, she stared at the monitor. She read her choices: "Word Processing Pro-

gram''; ''Spreadsheets''; ''Desktop Publishing''; ''Return
to DOS.''

Her eyes focused on the last. ''Return to DOS.'' Even her
computer was sending her a message.

It's amazing how fast you can reach the West Coast by air,
Becky thought. She had just completed her first plane ride.
Quite nicely, too. She left the airport quickly, her stomach
in knots over the prospect of seeing Dan again. Making her
way into the building that housed the Simmons Corporation she felt as though an army of butterflies had taken up
permanent residence in her stomach. Whatever happened,
she'd never be the same.

Was it too late? Had she thrown away the best thing that
had ever happened to her?

Knees knocking, Becky entered the elevator, punching the
button for the corporate floor, where she knew Dan's office had to be. The elevator whizzed to the designated place
and opened its doors. Before Becky could change her mind,
she pushed open the heavy mahogany door to the office.
Once inside, she let her eyes travel over the thick, plush, rose
carpeting, the handsome, white-upholstered chairs, the glass
coffee table and the original framed work of a well-known
artist. The entire room suggested wealth and prosperity.

Feeling out of place in her sensible navy midcalf skirt and
white blouse, Becky took a tentative step toward the receptionist. And stopped. Completely. The door on the other
side of the receptionist's desk had opened soundlessly.
Looking up, Becky met Dan's eyes. And time seemed to
stop.

''Becky.'' Dan's voice was a mere whisper as he studied
the woman he loved. He blinked. She was still there. How
he had missed her!

''Dan.'' Neither of them said anything else. Neither of
them moved.

He recovered first. ''Come in.'' Dan quietly ushered her
into his office.

Once he closed the door, Dan stared at Becky. They were an arm's length away from each other. Her nicely rehearsed speech of apology was frozen somewhere in her throat. The words he planned to say if she ever came back to him were forgotten.

Becky stared at the man who had become her life. The custom-tailored brown suit fit him perfectly. His pin-striped shirt was neatly pressed. The chocolate-brown tie and brown leather shoes complemented the outfit.

With a push of a button, he informed someone he'd be late getting to his next meeting. Several papers lay on his desk, awaiting his signature. Becky decided she'd never seen him look so authoritative, so completely in command. He had power and he knew how to use it. Could everything be the same between them?

"I've missed you." Her words were soft, faltering.

Dan smiled. Lord, she was here! And she was beautiful. "Becky," he began, "please say you've come back to me. Say you'll marry me." He walked over to her.

He was standing so close Becky could feel his breath on her face. In that moment she knew that somehow they'd be together.

"I want to, Dan, but I'm not sure I can fit into your world." She looked at him.

Dan groaned, reaching her, pulling her close. His mouth covered hers, and they both took what they needed.

After several long kisses, Dan drew back, his eyes shining. He smoothed a lock of her hair. "We'll make our own world if we have to. A world for us." He smiled softly at her. "All right?"

"Yes," Becky whispered, her eyes shining.

She had returned to DOS—the man she loved.

**Fifty red-blooded, white-hot, true-blue hunks
from every State in the Union!**

Look for MEN MADE IN AMERICA! Written by some of our most poplar authors, these stories feature fifty of the strongest, sexiest men, each from a different state in the union!

Two titles available every other month at your favorite retail outlet.

In January, look for:

DREAM COME TRUE by Ann Major (Florida)
WAY OF THE WILLOW by Linda Shaw (Georgia)

In March, look for:

TANGLED LIES by Anne Stuart (Hawaii)
ROGUE'S VALLEY by Kathleen Creighton (Idaho)

You won't be able to resist MEN MADE IN AMERICA!

Relive the romance...
Harlequin and Silhouette
are proud to present

by Request™

A program of collections of three complete novels by the most requested authors with the most requested themes. Be sure to look for one volume each month with three complete novels by top name authors.

In January: **WESTERN LOVING**   Susan Fox
                                         JoAnn Ross
                                         Barbara Kaye

Loving a cowboy is easy—taming him isn't!

In February: **LOVER, COME BACK!**   Diana Palmer
                                           Lisa Jackson
                                         Patricia Gardner Evans

It was over so long ago—yet now they're calling, "Lover, Come Back!"

In March: **TEMPERATURE RISING**   JoAnn Ross
                                         Tess Gerritsen
                                       Jacqueline Diamond

Falling in love—just what the doctor ordered!

Available at your favorite retail outlet.

REQ-G3

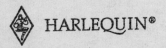

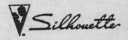

NEW YORK TIMES **Bestselling Author**

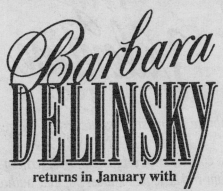

Barbara DELINSKY

returns in January with

THE REAL THING

Stranded on an island off the coast of Maine,
Deirdre Joyce and Neil Hersey got the
solitude they so desperately craved—
but they also got each other, something they
hadn't expected. Nor had they expected
to be consumed by a desire so powerful
that the idea of living alone again was
unimaginable. A marrige of "convenience"
made sense—or did it?   BOB7

HARLEQUIN®